Don't Water Marigolds

By
James Sinclair

Don't Water the Marigolds

By James Sinclair

This book or any portion thereof may not be reproduced or used in any manner whatsoever without the express written permission of the publisher except for the use of brief quotations in a book review.

The purchaser of this book is subject to the condition that he/she shall in no way resell it, nor any part of it, nor make copies of it to distribute freely.

This book is a work of fiction. Any similarity between the characters and situations within its pages and places or persons, living or dead, is unintentional and coincidental.

Text Copyright © 2014
James Sinclair

All Rights Reserved

Other books by James Sinclair

Over Our Heads

Table of Contents

Chapter 1
Chapter 2
Chapter 3
Chapter 4
Chapter 5
Chapter 6
Chapter 7
Chapter 8
Chapter 9
Chapter 10
Chapter 11
Chapter 12
Chapter 13
Chapter 14
Chapter 15
Chapter 16
Chapter 17
Chapter 18
Chapter 19
Chapter 20
Chapter 21
Chapter 22
Chapter 23
Chapter 24
About the Author

Don't Water The Marigolds
By James Sinclair

Chapter 1

The doorbell rang. Deirdre Hinton, dozing in her armchair with an open book on her lap, awoke with a start. She placed the book on the small side table, careful to put the bookmark on the open page. Then, she closed the book, and rose to her feet, quite energetically for her age, and not needing the armrests to lever herself up. She made her way to the front door, opened it a crack, and peered through. A young female stood on the threshold.

"Hi. I've come about the room," she said, through the gum she chewed.

Oh, the room. Deirdre had forgotten about the room. She had approached Social Services and informed them she had a room to let, preferably to a young working girl. This decision had been made after some careful deliberation. After all, here she was, living in a large house all by herself, while there were so many young people desperately looking for a place to live.

"You had better come inside, then," she said and opened

the door wider.

"I've just come from the Social," the girl said, "and my name is Sharon."

Deirdre took the girl in with one glance—a pale oval face with dark, lank hair. One lock dyed a bright scarlet. She wore dark lipstick—almost black, and had a stud in her nose and another just below her bottom lip. A pair of large earrings dangled from each ear. A tattoo adorned one side of her neck, and both her upper arms. She was, apparently, in her mid-twenties, but dressed more like a teenager—mutton dressed up as lamb, Deirdre thought.

"Oh, I see. Yes, the room is upstairs," she said. "Please do come in and I'll show it to you." The girl crossed over the threshold and her high heels tap-tapped on the hardwood floor.

"You'd better go up first, Dear," she said. "You have younger legs." The girl climbed up the stairs and waited on the landing for Deirdre.

"It's the room on the right," Deirdre said.

The girl opened the door and Deirdre followed her in. The room was large and airy, with a window at one end. A bed with fresh linen and a quilt stood against one wall. A washstand, complete with porcelain washbasin, soap dish and water-jug, lived in one corner, while an old-fashioned dressing table with a large oval mirror stood in another corner. A chest of drawers and a hanging wardrobe completed the furnishings.

The girl took these in in one glance. "I suppose it will have to do," she said. "But there is something I have to say first. I'm a single mum and have a nine-year old son. Is that a problem?"

"Ah. I think it might be, Dear." Deirdre hadn't reckoned on having a child in the house. "The room is for single tenancy only," she said. "I thought Social Services would have made you aware of that."

A look of disappointment passed over the girl's face, and the corners of her plump lips turned downward. "Well, they know I have a child, and they didn't say anything." She snapped her gum.

A wave of sympathy passed over Deirdre. So difficult, she thought, with single mothers these days—what with all the shortage of accommodation.

"You couldn't possibly share the room with your young son, but," she added impulsively, "there might be a solution. You see, I have another small bedroom where your young son may be able to stay—what's his name?"

"Kevin."

"Of course," Deirdre continued, "it's still filled up with rubbish, but it can always be cleared out. Come this way, and I'll show it to you."

She led the girl along the upstairs balcony and opened the door to a small room, cluttered up with bits and pieces—mainly old books and household junk. A window sat at one end with a skylight above.

"Of course, it will have to be redecorated and furnished. I have some bits and pieces in the garage, and it only means getting a bed."

"This will do fine," the girl said. "Can we talk about the rent and other things?"

"Come downstairs, Dear. But, you'd better see the bathroom and toilet first, while we're upstairs. There's a separate bathroom and toilet, and there is a shower fitted over the tub. Most people prefer to shower these days, don't you agree?"

Downstairs again, in the kitchen, Deirdre asked, "Would you like a cup of tea, Dear?"

"Coffee." The girl snapped her gum, again.

"Right you are. Coffee it is. As you can see, I have had the kitchen modernised recently, by a friend who is a builder and decorator. He's done a good job, don't you think?"

"It looks fine."

"And there is a washing machine and a small dishwasher. So convenient these days."

She filled a whistling type kettle with water from the tap and placed it on the electric hob.

"Let's go into the front room while it boils. Then we can talk about the rent and things."

"Do you allow smoking?"

"Not in the house, Dear. Though, you can always smoke in the conservatory, or on the patio. There's a small bench there where you can sit. I used to smoke in the old days, you know, but I gave it up years ago. So bad for your health, they say."

They sat in the front room whilst they discussed the rent and house rules. Then the kettle whistled and Deirdre left the girl and returned a little later with two mugs of steaming coffee.

"I get help from the Social, with the rent."

"Do you not have a job?"

"Yes. I work in a flower shop in the village. The pay's not too good, but it's a job and, with help from the Social, I manage to get by — for myself and Kev."

"What school does he go to?"

"Holyfield — just a mile or so down the road from here."

"I know it well. In fact, I used to teach there when I was young," Deirdre said. "But not the younger children. Just the older girls and boys."

"I see. So, you were a teacher?"

"Oh, yes, for many years. Then, later, I used to lecture at one of the universities — in Cambridge, you know."

The girl eyed Deirdre but said nothing, just continued chewing her gum.

"So you see, I am quite used to children," Deirdre continued, "and I get along with them very well. I am sure Kevin and I will be good friends."

"They can be a handful," the girl said with a glum look, then added, "but Kev's a good boy."

"I'm sure he is, Dear."

"You won't mind having a kid about the house?"

"Good heavens, no. I enjoy young company. It keeps you young, you know. And one does miss not having grandchildren."

"Do you have an Internet connection?"

"Oh no, Dear. I don't understand computers at all."

"Kev's always on his laptop."

"Well, I'm sure something can always be arranged. I do understand that young children these days are rather addicted to their computers."

There was a long awkward silence, and then Deirdre said, "By the way, I have a cat." She nodded towards the sofa, where a large ginger tom lay asleep on a cushion. "His name is Timothy. Would he be a problem for you or for Kevin?"

"Naw," the girl said, "Kev loves animals. He's always pestering me to get one, but you know how it is with finding a place to stay and all."

"He doesn't suffer from any allergies?"

"He's not asthmatic or anything, if that's what you mean," Sharon said. "But he can be hyperactive at times, which is a bit of a pain."

"Oh—most children are. They never seem to be able to sit still for a moment. We used to call it fidgeting in the old days."

"It's boredom."

"Yes, children these days seem to get bored so easily. In our day, we always used to find something to do, even if it were just reading a book. I don't suppose children read very much these days?"

"Kev likes Harry Potter."

"And who is he, Dear?"

"You haven't heard of Harry Potter — the books written by J.K. Rowling?" Sharon gave her an incredulous look.

"Oh, *that* Harry Potter. Now that you mention it, yes, Dear, I have. I'm not completely out-of-touch with the modern world. Wasn't he some sort of boy wizard?"

"Yes. He's mad about Harry Potter."

"Well, Dear," Deirdre said, "I think we have covered most things. It's just Kevin's room that needs to be sorted out. When would you like to move in?"

"As soon as his room is ready," Sharon said, but she didn't sound enthusiastic — just bored. "If that's okay with you?"

"I'll get on to it immediately. Do you have a phone on

which I can contact you?"

"I have my mobile," Sharon said. She foraged around in her handbag and found it, checked the number, then read it out to Deirdre who, after searching for a scrap of paper and a pencil, wrote it down.

"I'll give you my number in case you need to contact me," Deirdre said. She called it out from memory while Sharon keyed it in on her mobile.

They both got up and Deirdre saw Sharon to the door.

"Well, I'll wait to hear from you — about Kev's room I mean," Sharon said as she left with a "ta-ra" and a wave of her hand.

"Goodbye, Dear," Deirdre said to her back, as she watched Sharon walk down the path and through the gate. She closed the front door and went straight to the kitchen and put the kettle on to boil again. A welcome cup of tea, this time — none of that coffee malarkey.

Her mind was in a whirl, now filled with doubt. Was she doing the right thing? After all, having a lodger was fine. She had thought about it long and hard, and although she didn't really need the rent money, she considered that a lodger — preferably a young working girl — would be company for her in this large, empty house. But, to take on one with a young child! Was she completely mad? It all seemed to have happened so quickly, and caught her on the wrong foot. What made her agree so impulsively to have a child in the house? Despite what she had told Sharon, what did she really know about children anyway?

Her last experience with the modern day young was when, one day, she'd decided the local stream, the 'Spode,' that ran down at the end of the lane, needed tidying up. She had seen the litter thrown in the stream — empty Coke cans, beer bottles and other rubbish. Armed with black bin-bags, she went down to the stream again, determined to tidy it up. Three little boys were there this time, idly throwing stones into the stream. She approached them.

"Now, Dears," she said. "This is our little stream and, as

you can see, it is in an awful mess. So, I would like you to gather up all the empty bottles and cans and put them into these bags. Our environment is very precious to us you know, so you can see the need for tidying up the stream and putting all the cans and bottles into bags for recycling."

One of the little boys turned and looked at her. "Fuck off."

Deirdre returned to the front room with a cup of tea in her hand. Timothy the cat looked up at her from the cushion on the sofa, yawned, and stretched.
She sat down in her armchair, and in a moment, Timothy jumped up on her lap.

"Oh, Timothy," she said, "your Mummy is a silly old lady." She stroked his head while he purred. She must ring Social Services, she thought, and find out a bit more about this young lady, Sharon, who she was about to admit into her home. After all, she knew nothing about her background, and at the time, she had felt too timid to pry.

The girl was obviously unmarried. But, did she have a boyfriend? Mildred, her long-standing Jamaican friend who held a senior position in the Social Services, would tell her more about Sharon. Deirdre was quite involved with Social Services, as she had done some work for them in the past. I won't ask just now, she thought. She must get her mind in order first. At the moment, it was in confusion.

She got up from her chair, pushed a disgruntled Timothy off, and went to the drinks cabinet. She got hold of the bottle of Scotch, and poured a generous measure into her tea — 'tiger's milk,' Howard always called it.

Her thoughts returned to the girl. Her attire suggested that she might be a bit flighty. Was she going to be troublesome? Was Deirdre taking on too much? A young woman, of unknown background, and a young child to boot! Was the girl on drugs? She certainly smoked. Would she have a boyfriend in her bedroom? Deirdre wracked her brain to try to remember what she had told Sharon about house rules.

Despite her sixty-five years, Deirdre was rather liberal and broad-minded, but she drew the line at drugs and was uncomfortable with sleep-in boyfriends.

A walk would clear her mind. So, she donned her cloak and scarf, covering her long Viyella gown, which was printed with a Paisley pattern. It came down to her calves. A seamstress always made Deirdre's clothes, as she could never find what she wanted in the shops—not even Marks. She was a short person, only about five feet two0 inches in height, and had a small, heart-shaped, cheerful face and a fresh complexion with hardly a wrinkle in sight. Customarily, she wore her grey hair fastened back in an untidy bun.

She walked down to the 'Spode,' and tried to clear the thoughts whirling around in her brain.

Was it loneliness that made her agree to have a child in the house? Yes, she had been lonely, she admitted. Howard and she had never had any children, and as a consequence, had been deprived of any grandchildren too. Oh, how she missed him—his steadying hand and sound advice. "Get hold of yourself, girl," he would say, whenever she acted impulsively — as she was doing now.

What if the boy was unruly and badly behaved? She imagined him bumping into, and smashing, her precious ornaments. The girl had said he was hyperactive. Why, oh why, had she agreed to it? Why had she been so accommodating as to suggest the small spare bedroom for Kevin? She should have said at the outset that she couldn't have a child in the house. But, what was done, was done, she thought regretfully. She'd have to wait and see what Mildred had to say about Sharon. With these thoughts in her mind, she returned home to a waiting Timothy.

Chapter 2

The next couple of weeks passed busily for Deirdre. She phoned Mildred at the Social Services, who told her that Sharon Clarke had been on their books for some time, and that there was nothing adverse about her character — not on drugs or anything.

Then Deirdre called in her builder-decorator, Dave, to come and have a look at the room, to see if it needed re-decorating.

Dave rubbed his chin as he surveyed the cluttered space. "Well, the wallpaper will have to be stripped for a start, and the floor needs re-carpeting." He dropped his hands to his hips, "What are you going to do about the furniture? No one has a wash-stand in their bedroom, these days." He gave her an amused smile.

"It has been like this since Howard's mother moved into the care home. Even after she died, we just never got around to doing anything with it. And, now Howard is gone . . ."

"You ought to get some more modern furniture," he said. "Most of the stuff you have went out with the Ark!" They shared a chuckle.

Deirdre wasn't mean. She did agree that the room needed refurbishing, and Dave suggested a new bed and white modern furniture to brighten things up. "I'll bring over some catalogues for you to see and you can choose."

For Kevin's room, he said he would have the clutter removed and perhaps stored away in the garage or loft, and also suggested what furniture would be suitable for a nine-year-old's bedroom. He should know, Deirdre thought, seeing as he had a son about Kevin's age.

So, finally, the work went ahead with much hammering, drilling and sawing. When the rooms were finished, she viewed the results with satisfaction. They looked clean and bright and the smell of fresh paint hung in the air. Of course, it had been an expense, but she reckoned that with the rent she received each month her investment would soon be recovered.

She rang Sharon on her mobile, and informed her that the rooms were now ready and she could move in whenever she wished.

A few days later, a white van arrived with Sharon and a little boy and all their chattels.

"This is Kevin," Sharon said, when Deirdre met them at the door.

"How do you do?" Deirdre said, as she took Kevin's moist little hand and shook it solemnly.

"Say 'hello' to Mrs Hinton."

"Oh, please. Just call me Deirdre. Everyone else does."

"Hello …" He hesitated, "De-De."

"Yes, 'De-De' will do very nicely," Deidre said. "It's a difficult name to pronounce."

He looked to be a small boy, even for his nine years, with dark straight hair and grey eyes. Freckles peppered his face, and he had a dimple on his chin.

"You must come upstairs and see the rooms again," Deirdre said. "I have just had them redecorated and the furniture changed. My workman has done a splendid job."

They went upstairs while the van driver set about unloading the cardboard boxes from the van.

"Wow!" Sharon exclaimed as she viewed the room.

"Yes, it has made a difference, don't you agree?" Deirdre said. "Everything looks so much brighter."

"It's fabulous," Sharon said. "But you shouldn't have gone to all the trouble and expense."

"It needed doing. Now, come along and have a look at Kevin's room."

It was Kevin's turn. "Awesome," he said as he stood at the doorway.

Dave had done a good job.

The room had been re-papered, and posters of comic-book superheroes had been Blue-Tacked onto the walls. There was even one of 'Harry Potter and the Philosopher's Stone.'

The bed-cover had pictures of sports cars, and a desk sat near the window, next to a white chest-of drawers with a mirror above. Shelves had been erected on the walls, and every inch of available space had been cleverly utilised.

"Where shall I put these?" the van driver asked as he struggled up the steps with a cardboard box.

"Oh, just leave them on the floor of that bedroom," Sharon said. She pointed in the relevant direction. "Kev, give the man a hand with some of the boxes."

Kevin raced down the stairs.

"I'm sure you're ready for a cup of tea now," Deirdre said. "Or would you prefer coffee?"

"A cup of coffee will be fine."

"What about Kevin?"

"Oh, just a can of Coke or something."

"I don't have any Coke," Deirdre said. "Would orange juice do?"

Sharon gave her a doubtful look. "Fine."

"Have you had anything to eat? Can I make you a

sandwich or something?"

"No, we've already eaten," Sharon said.

"Right. Would you like it downstairs?"

"That'll be fine. I'll come down with you."

They waited for Kevin, struggling with a cardboard box, to come up the stairs before going down the stairway.

Deirdre felt happier in her mind now, as she boiled the kettle, and Sharon waited in the front room. Most of her apprehension assuaged as she became more accustomed to the idea of sharing her home with two strangers.

Kevin seemed a well-behaved and polite little boy, and Sharon — once you accepted her appearance — seemed quite pleasant. One mustn't judge by appearances, she thought. It was like judging a book by its cover.

During the course of her life and experience, she had learned not to be too judgmental. She had always been a Liberal, and sometimes she and Howard argued furiously over their different points-of-view, he being a staunch Conservative.

Of course, she and Howard had come from completely different backgrounds. His parents had been terrible snobs, especially his father, a cabinet-maker, who would always have an ear-trumpet stuck in his ear and say "Eh? Eh? What's that you said?" and slam down his newspaper and leave the room if he disagreed. Howard's mother had been more genteel, but a snob nevertheless.

Deirdre entered with a tray. "Here's your coffee, Dear, and a drink for Kevin." Sharon didn't offer any help, as Deirdre bent to set the tray down on the table. "And there are some chocolate-chip biscuits. Does Kevin like chocolate?"

"He loves it and he'll eat anything," Sharon said, with what was becoming a familiar bored look. "*Kev—*"she shouted. "Come in and have a drink and some biscuits, Mrs Hinton … err … Deirdre, has brought for you."

"Coming!" A rush of footsteps sounded down the stairway, and Kevin entered the room short of breath. "Those boxes are fuc … err … bloomin' heavy."

"Yes, Dear. You mustn't strain yourself," Deirdre said.

"Let the man carry them up. At least the heavy ones. I am sure he can manage on his own."

Kevin eyed his glass. "Don't you have any Coke?" he asked.

"No. I'm afraid not, Dear," Deirdre said.

"Drink up your juice and don't make a fuss," Sharon said in a sharp tone.

Kevin shrugged, took a sip, and bit into a chocolate-chip biscuit.

"When do his school holidays start?" Deirdre asked.

"Not for a month or so," Sharon said. "This may be a problem, because I might not get time off from work, and I can't afford to go away and take Kevin on holiday anywhere."

Deirdre saw the next question coming.

"Would it be too much of a cheek if I asked you to keep an eye on him when he's home?"

"Does he not have any uncles or anyone he could spend some time with?"

"No. Nobody."

An awkward silence fell for a moment as Deirdre stared into her cup of tea. Here it was. Again, the same weakness. Fortunately, the van driver poking his head around the door interrupted them.

"All the stuff's upstairs now."

"Excuse me," Sharon said. She gathered her purse and accompanied the man to the front door. Deirdre heard some argument, then the sound of the front door closing. Sharon re-entered the room.

"Do you mind if I go outside for a fag?"

"Not at all, Dear. You can smoke in the conservatory or in the garden, if you wish."

"I'll have a wander round the garden."

Deirdre was grateful for the break. It would give her some time to think. But Kevin interrupted her thoughts.

"What's that funny thing on the mantelpiece?"

"It's a clock, Dear."

"It's a funny looking clock."

"Yes, it is rather unusual. It's in the art deco style. A

friend of mine made it. He's an artist who specialises in art deco."

"What's art deco?"

"Oh, it's an art style that flourished between the 1920s and '40s. A long while ago now, Dear—even for an old biddy like me."

"You must be pretty ancient, then."

"I'm sixty-five, but yes, to someone of your age, I suppose that's pretty old—or as you say, ancient."

"I don't know any old people."

"Well, meeting me will be your first experience," Deirdre said with a bright smile. "I hope we'll be friends."

"Yeah." Kevin fidgeted. "Do you like frogs?" he asked, spotting an ornament among other bric-a-brac in a glass-fronted cabinet.

"Why, yes, Dear. I have a frog in the garden. He sometimes sits on the lily pad in the little pond. I like all nature's little creatures."

"Is he there now?"

"I don't think so."

"I kept a frog once," Kevin said. "I mean, he wasn't a frog when I first got him. He was just a tiddly tadpole, about so big." He indicated the size with his fingers. "I kept him in a goldfish bowl, and then suddenly he sprouted legs and his tail fell off, and then he became a frog and hopped away."

"Ah. That's one of nature's many miracles," Deirdre said, "watching a tadpole grow into a frog. It's something that you can witness day by day, as you did. Another of nature's marvels is when a hairy caterpillar changes into a beautiful butterfly. But of course, you can't see it changing, because it's in its chrysalis. But when that splits open, a butterfly emerges. It's a process called metamorphosis."

"Oh, I get it," Kevin said. "It's when something morphs into something else. I have some toys that do that."

"Yes, Dear. But it's not entirely the same thing."

Sharon came back into the room, and brought a smell of smoke with her. "I guess we'd better go upstairs and start unpacking. Come on, Kev."

"Yes, Dear, I expect you will want to get settled in. Kevin and I have been having such an interesting conversation about metamorphosis."

Sharon stared back at her with a blank look.

They both went back upstairs. Now, at last, she would have time to think about the question Sharon had posed to her. She still had half a cup of tea left in her teacup, and took it to the drinks cabinet and poured in a tot of whisky from the bottle. More tiger's milk was called for.

What was she going to say? Did Sharon expect her to look after Kevin during the school holidays? Obviously, she did. Was she expected to become a glorified baby-sitter for Kevin? The thought irked her. She hated being taken advantage of, and being such a soft fool. Her weakness angered her. But then, she reflected, she *had* enjoyed chatting to Kevin. Perhaps it wouldn't be too bad an idea. After all, she had a lot of time on her hands, and to have someone to talk to would fill the vacant hours, and Kevin seemed a bright and chatty child, not sullen or withdrawn. She took a large gulp of tiger's milk, and felt its warm glow reach her stomach.

Deirdre sat in her armchair and reflected. What had she achieved in her lifetime? Yes, she had made a few accomplishments, and fortunately too, Howard had left her quite well-off. But what had she actually *done* with her life? What contribution to society had she made?

Of course, she had received some recognition for charitable work she had done to help raise funds for the NSPCC in the past.

But otherwise, when she passed on there would be little to remember her by. She had not even written a book, which she had always wanted to do. Yes, her career in teaching had been rewarding, and she had been happy in her marriage with Howard, but they had never contemplated having children, so she had no one even to inherit her property.

Perhaps this situation was giving her an opportunity to do something good in her life. Heaven knows, if she had her time over again, she would have probably gone out to some country like Africa or India and done some charitable work.

She felt somehow that her life had lacked purpose. Being a great believer in karma, she believed what good you did in this life would be rewarded in another incarnation.

She heard Sharon coming down the stairs, then she popped her head round the doorway. "I have some groceries to put away," she said. "Could you show me where to keep them?"

Deirdre led her into the kitchen. "You can put your stores away in this cabinet," she said.

"And you can keep your fresh food in these two compartments in the fridge. You can also store any frozen food in the middle two compartments of the freezer." She pointed to a row of gleaming copper pots and pans. "And you can use any of these utensils that you wish. The plates and things are all in this cabinet."

It was a large and spacious kitchen, and all the appliances were modern and up-to-date, including a large fridge-freezer and microwave oven. A table and four chairs stood in the centre of the room.

"You can have your meals here, if you wish," Deirdre said.

"Or you can use the dining room whenever you like. I usually take my meals in the kitchen."

"I'll go down to the shops a bit later," Sharon said. "I'll catch the bus that goes into the village."

"I can take you in my little car. It will save you carrying back heavy shopping on the bus."

"S'all right," Sharon said. "Kev will come with me to help."

"As you please, Dear," Deirdre said. "But it's no trouble. It's the 265 bus you want. The bus stop is just past the gate, and it stops in the village opposite Budgen's."

"Yes, I know." Sharon shifted from foot to foot, in evident impatience.

Deirdre left her to put away her groceries — mostly dried foodstuffs.

A while later, Sharon, with Kevin in tow, left the house, and Deirdre settled herself in her armchair and continued with her book. But she couldn't concentrate. Perhaps another tot of Scotch? Straight from the bottle this time!

Chapter 3

The next evening, Sharon and Kevin joined Deirdre in the living room.

"You don't mind if we sit with you and watch a bit of telly?" Sharon asked.

"Not at all, Dears. You are most welcome." She switched on the television from the remote and handed it to Sharon. "Please feel free to watch anything you wish."

Deirdre had invested in a large modern LCD television with Freeview built in. She had had to get rid of her old box-type television set when the digital switchover happened, as her old Ferguson wasn't capable of receiving the new signal. She didn't regret it, but still watched only the five original channels.

"Do you mind if I put on 'East-Enders'?"

"Please feel free to do so," Deirdre said.

"I was an avid fan of Coronation Street in the old days, you know. But I haven't been keeping up with the series and I'm afraid I'm a bit out-of-touch with all the new characters now."

"Can I watch Sponge-Bob Square-Pants after that, Mum?"

"You can if that's okay with Deirdre."

"Who is Sponge-Bob Square—whoever?" Deirdre asked.

"Oh, Sponge-Bob?" Kevin said. "He's a sponge and because he's square, he wears square pants, so that's why he's called Sponge-Bob Square-Pants. It's a really cool program."

Sharon looked at Deirdre. "Kids will watch anything."

"Yes, I know, Dear. It was Donald Duck and Mickey Mouse in my day. Things have changed so much. I'll leave you dears to enjoy your television whilst I make myself some supper and feed Timothy. Have you had yours?"

"Yeah—just a snack," Sharon said.

Deirdre left them, followed by Timothy, who seemed to know instinctively when it was feeding-time.

In the kitchen, she fed Timothy from a pouch of Whiskas cat food, and then made herself some cheese-on-toast and a cup of hot Bovril to go with it. She switched on the TV in the kitchen. Again, Dave had thoughtfully suggested a kitchen

TV and installed it on a bracket for her. He was a good man. She watched 'The Antiques Road Show' on BBC whilst she ate her cheese-on-toast and sipped her Bovril.

How was it going to work out? she wondered, with these two new people living in her house. She had become so accustomed to being on her own all these years since Howard departed, that she was conscious of the invasion of her privacy and space.

She finished her snack and popped the dirty plate and cup into the dishwasher. Then Sharon came into the kitchen.

"Would you mind very much keeping an eye on Kevin while I pop into the pub for a drink?"

Here it was — the start of the baby-sitting duties! What would Sharon have done if she and Kevin were living by themselves?

But instead, Deirdre said, "Of course, I don't mind! There's the 'Soldier of Fortune' just down the road. It's a quiet pub and the publican is a good friend of mine."

"Thanks a bunch," Sharon said. "Could you see Kev gets to

bed before nine o'clock? Once he's in front of the goggle-box, he'll watch it for hours on end."

"I will do precisely that," Deirdre said. "You go and enjoy yourself, Dear."

"I'll be back in an hour or two. Oh, and would you mind tucking him in? He's gotten used to that."

"Goodness—I've never done that before, tucking a child into bed. But I'll give it a go."

"Yeah, thanks. And he usually likes a bedtime story."

"I'll try my best. Does he have any story books?"

"Yeah. He unpacked some of them today and put them on the shelves. I hope you don't think this too much of a cheek," she said with a note of apology in her voice.

"Not at all, Dear." The old weakness again! Why was she finding it so difficult to simply say 'No'?

Sharon left the kitchen and Deirdre heard her going upstairs, and then, about ten minutes later, she came down again, in her high-heels. The front door closed.

Responsibility. Deirdre sighed and clenched her fingers

together. She had never been answerable for anything much over the last few years, excepting herself, and of course, Timothy. Although a cat hardly requires any dependability as they are such independent creatures. Now, here she was, taking on responsibility again, after all these years. Suppose Kevin played up and refused to go to bed? What authority did she have over him? Was she strong enough to cope with such a situation?

With a shake of her head, she returned to the lounge. Kevin lay sprawled on his stomach on the floor, watching the TV. Deirdre glanced at the clock. It was half-past eight.

"Did you watch your Sponge-Bob-whatever program?"

"Nah," Kevin said. "You can't get it on your TV."

"Oh, what a pity. Your Mum has gone out for a while, Kevin dear," she said. "She'll be back a bit later, but she's asked me to make sure you're in bed before nine o'clock."

"Okey-doke, De-De." Kevin gave her a brief glance, then returned his attention to the TV. "Just let me finish watching this program. It ends at nine."

His acquiescence came as a relief. Deirdre had half-expected him to make a fuss. She sat down in her armchair, put on her glasses and picked up her book. Timothy sat at her feet, licking his paws contentedly.

True to his word, Kevin switched off the TV as the clock struck nine. "I'm going to bed now," he said. "Are you coming up to tuck me in?"

"Yes, of course, Dear. You go upstairs first and get undressed and I'll be up shortly."

"I have to brush my teeth first. Mum always makes me brush my teeth before bed."

"A very good habit, I'm sure."

He left the room and she heard his footsteps going up the stairs. About ten minutes later, he called out from the landing, "De-De. I'm ready for bed now."

Upstairs, she found Kevin dressed in his pyjama suit and sitting on his bed with a book in his hands.

"You have to tuck me in now," he said, crawling under the covers. "This bed is really cool. I love sports cars."

"I'm so glad you're pleased," Deirdre said. "My workman, Dave, took no end of trouble doing up your room for you. He has a nine-year-old son just like you, and he knows what boys of your age like."

It was a completely new experience for her as she tucked Kevin into bed, and a strange warm feeling passed over her.

"Read to me from this page," Kevin said, and handed her the book. It was 'Harry Potter and the Philosopher's Stone', and the cover was very similar to the poster Dave had thoughtfully fixed to the wall.

"I can read for myself, you know," Kevin said. "But I like someone reading to me."

"Very well, Dear." Deirdre sat on the edge of the bed and put her glasses on the end of her nose. She read in her clear, precise voice. But had only covered a couple of pages when she noticed Kevin was fast asleep.

Carefully, she closed the book and left it on the bedside table. Then she switched off the bedside light and exited the room. She left the door ajar, to let in some light from the landing.

Well, that was that, she thought, success. She felt quite proud of herself. Except when she taught them at school, she had never had much to do with children, and that was in a more formal environment than this.

The only time she had had some experience looking after a small child was when, some time back, her neighbour had asked her to take charge of her four-year-old boy for the afternoon while she had some business to do in Cambridge.

Rather than sit with him in the house, Deirdre had taken him out berry-picking.

They were quite a distance out in the fields where blackberry bushes grew in profusion, and they proceeded to pick the juicy berries and place them in the wicker basket Deirdre carried. Suddenly, the boy announced that he needed to go to the toilet.

"Go behind the bushes, Dear, and have a wee."

"No. I'se got to do number two."

"Well, go behind them anyway, Dear," she said.

The boy disappeared behind the bushes, while Deirdre continued with her berry picking. A short time later, his little voice said, "You'se got to wipe me, now." She turned around and was presented with a little pink bottom pointing up at her.

Deirdre returned to the living room and switched on the television. She watched the news, then 'Newsnight'. There was some political interview going on with Jeremy Paxman.

The voices droned on and lulled her into a doze. The key being turned in the front door awoke her, and a moment later, Sharon poked her head into the living room.

"Kev in bed?" she asked.

"Yes, Dear," Deirdre said, and rose to her feet. "He was no trouble at all."

"That's a change. Usually he makes a fuss at bedtime." Sharon remained on the other side of the doorframe.

"Would you like a cup of tea — or something stronger?" Deirdre said with a glint in her eye.

"No, ta." Sharon took a step back, further into the hallway. "I've had more than my share at the pub." She giggled. "I'm off to bed now. Nighty-night."

"Goodnight, Dear," Deirdre said. "I'll be going up in a moment too."

Again, Deirdre sensed a feeling of warmth pass over her. Perhaps it wasn't going to be too bad after all, having company in the house.

Looking after Kevin had been a rewarding experience and she grudgingly admitted that she had enjoyed it.

Still with this glow of satisfaction, she got up from her chair and called out to her cat, "Come now, Timothy. Beddy-byes." He yawned, and with a purr jumped off the sofa and followed her upstairs.

Chapter 4

'Mayfield', where Deirdre lived, was a large, white detached house. It had a big front garden, surrounded by a privet hedge. A small pond graced the centre of the lawn and a rockery sat in one corner. The garden also boasted some fruit trees — mainly apples and pears, and some shrubs and bushes. A horse-chestnut tree stood at one corner of the garden, and a paved driveway led from a wrought-iron gate to a porch in front of the house, with a garage to one side.

Inside the house, a wide hallway led to the lounge and kitchen, and had steps on the right, which led upstairs to the landing. The kitchen was at the far end of the hallway. Near the front door was the living room, a large and spacious chamber, with bow windows in front. The dining room led off through an archway, and had a conservatory attached, with cane furniture and a profusion of potted plants. From there, a door opened onto a patio and a large back garden.

Upstairs, two large bedrooms led off from the landing — one in front, the other at the back, and Kevin's small room nestled in-between. A small toilet could be found along the landing, and a larger bathroom alongside.

Deirdre and Howard had bought the house many years ago, when they sold up his parent's house, after the old man had died. His aged mother then moved in to live with them. She and Howard had been happy in their new home. Howard was a professor of history and taught at one of the universities at Cambridge, while Deirdre taught at the local school. They both liked living in the country, as the dark night skies, away from city lights, afforded them a clear view of the stars, and Howard had a passion for astronomy, one of his many hobbies.

His death ten years before, from oesophageal cancer, had come as a terrible blow for Deirdre. The illness had been a long and painful one, and it was harrowing to see him deteriorate before her very eyes, day by day, until he was only a shadow of his former self.

They had been good companions, and had so many interests in common. The sexual aspect of their lives, she had to admit, had been rather lacking in passion, but they loved each other dearly and that is what really mattered. They were not particularly fond of children, and never contemplated starting a family. Both of them had been 'only children' and hadn't experienced family life with siblings. They never even had any uncles, aunts or cousins, so Deirdre was very much alone in her old age.

The weeks passed, and it was soon time for the school holidays. Sharon had again broached the subject of Deirdre looking after Kevin while she was at work, and of course, Deirdre had weakly accepted, as was her wont.

Her main concern was how to keep a child entertained throughout the day. Children got bored so easily these days. Perhaps she could take him for walks or drives through the countryside. Of course, there was always his computer to keep him occupied.

Deirdre had decided to have a satellite dish and a Broadband Internet connection installed at her expense. Sharon had offered to contribute, but Deirdre had declined, understanding the girl's financial situation, saying, "No, Dear. Let's just say it's my treat."

Howard would have had it done years ago, she thought. He always liked to keep up with the technology of the day. She also opted for a Sky connection for the TV, so that Kevin could watch programs like his precious Sponge-Bob. She had gotten a package deal from Sky from the leaflet that had come in through the letterbox. So, there should be plenty to entertain him at home, she thought. At the moment, he lay on the floor, playing a noisy computer game on the TV from some gadget he had.

"Would you like something to eat, Dear?" she asked.

"Yeah," he said without looking up. "Just some chips." After a pause, he added, "Please."

"Would you like some baked beans with it and perhaps a fried egg?"

"Naw. Just the chips—and some tomato sauce."

Deirdre went to the kitchen and opened the freezer compartment. In Sharon's portion she found a large family pack of McCain oven chips. Chips, she thought. That was all children seemed to want to eat, these days. And burgers—McDonald's ones. No wonder obesity was so commonplace among the young.

She noticed that Sharon's concept of a healthy diet was sadly lacking. Largely ready-meals she could prepare in the microwave. The girl seldom gave him fresh fruit or vegetables.

It was the introduction of freezers, Deirdre concluded, that was largely to blame. She put the oven on to pre-heat and scattered a single layer of frozen potato chips on a baking tray. When she was a child, and they came from India to live in England, she remembered her mother preparing everything from scratch. She recalled helping her shell peas. Now everything came frozen. You hardly ever saw fresh peas in their pods at the greengrocers.

Of course, Deirdre had to admit, she herself bought ready-meals from the food-store in the village. Although she was an excellent cook and enjoyed cooking, she hardly bothered anymore. It was simply a question of convenience, saving all the trouble of boiling and mashing potatoes, for example, when it was so much quicker and easier to prepare the ready-made variety. Of course, living on her own and cooking for herself was unrewarding. Cooking for guests, or someone else, was so much more gratifying. One of these days, she would cook a meal for Sharon and Kevin, she decided, and give them a proper home-cooked meal.

Once the oven was at the right temperature, she popped in the baking tray, and made herself a tuna sandwich and a cup of soup while the chips were baking. She took these into the living room on a tray when they were ready. It would be useless to call Kevin into the kitchen. He was too engrossed in his computer game.

"Thank you," he said as he lay on the floor with his gadget. He broke off from furiously punching buttons on the games console, took the plate from her, and placed it on the floor beside him.

Deirdre gave him a wink, then sat in the armchair, the tray on her lap, and ate her sandwich, with sips of soup in-between.

"Would you like to come for a walk, Kevin?"

"Naw. Not really."

"It's a lovely sunny afternoon."

"Naw." He munched on a chip.

"The fresh air and sunshine will do you good," Deirdre insisted. "I can show you where the kingfisher lives near the stream. He often sits on a branch, and then dives into the water to catch a fish."

"Really?" He looked up, and interest lit up his features.

So, he *does* like animals, she mused. "Yes, and there are other things. Perhaps we could look for a newt in a pond and bring it back home in a jam-jar."

"That would be really cool," Kevin said and shoved another chip into his mouth, then switched off his computer game.

"Well, finish off your chips and get ready then."

It did not take Kevin long to complete this task. He gobbled them up at light-speed and handed the empty plate to Deirdre, who patted his head, placed the crockery on the tray, and took it into the kitchen.

Meanwhile, Kevin ran upstairs to put on his trainers.

"Better put your windcheater on, Dear. Although it's sunny outside, it's still a bit chilly."

Kevin obeyed, whilst Deirdre donned her cloak and scarf. They left the house, Kevin carrying an empty jam-jar in one hand and a large sieve from the kitchen in the other.

"Do you really think we'll find a newt?" he said, and skipped with excitement. "I've never had a newt. Just a frog."

"I'm sure we'll find one, Dear, if we know where to look. They're plenty about, this time of year."

They exited the gate, and walked down the lane to where the 'Spode' ran. The kingfisher was nowhere in sight, and although they waited, it never made an appearance.

"Let's look for the newt, De-De."

"We might find one in the stream," Deirdre said. "Although they prefer to live in ponds."

They peered into the water in vain.

"There's a little pond further up through the woods," Deirdre said. "Shall we try there?"

She led the way down a shady path and, after a ten-minute walk, they came to a little pond. It took them about a quarter-of-an-hour before they finally spotted a newt. Carefully, Kevin dipped the sieve into the water. "Got him!" he exclaimed and did an excited jig.

"Put it in the jar, quickly," Deirdre said.

Kevin picked up the slippery creature with his fingers and placed it carefully in the jam-jar filled with water. Then he held the jam-jar up and peered at the newt through the glass.

"Gosh—he's really awesome," Kevin said, and the wonderment showed in his tone of voice.

"Well, let's take him home, quickly," Deirdre said. "We

can keep him in the pond in the garden. He'll be good company for the little frog."

"Can't I keep him in the bottle for a few days?"

"I think he would feel more at home in the pond."

"Pleeease, De-De. Just for a few days?"

"Very well then," Deirdre said. "As long as your mother doesn't mind."

However, Sharon did mind.

"Ugh! It's really gross," she said as Kevin held up the jam-jar to her eye-level. "Don't bring it anywhere near me."

"I think he's really cool," Kevin said with a hint of disappointment in his voice. "De-De says I can keep him in the jam-jar in my bedroom for a few days."

"You're not having that thing in your bedroom," she said. "I'm sure it's unhealthy."

"Just for one night, Mum."

"Not for a night. Not ever," Sharon said. "It's like that horrible frog you had."

He ran down the steps to Deirdre, who had been listening

in the kitchen, with tears of anger and frustration rolling down his cheeks.

"Mum's not letting me keep him in my room," he said in a bitter tone and swiped at a tear with the back of his fist.

Deirdre patted his head. "Perhaps he'd be better off in the pond anyway, Dear. She won't have to look at him then, and you can visit him every day."

"She never lets me keep any pets," he said, obviously still angry. "Not even a beetle."

Deirdre wiped her hands on a kitchen towel. "Come now." She rested her hand on his shoulder. "Let's take him to the pond and put him in. I'm sure he'll be happy there."

They went out into the garden. Kevin tipped the water from the jam-jar into the pond, newt and all, and it swam hurriedly away.

"*You* like him, don't you, De-De?"

"I think he's very handsome indeed," Deirdre said, in an effort to comfort the distraught boy.

Kevin placed his hand in hers, which she squeezed, and they walked back to the house together.

Chapter 5

The school holidays passed busily for Deirdre and Kevin. When he was not on his computer or playing computer games on his X-Box, they went out for walks, and drives in the car. There was Bird World a couple of hour's drive away, and Deirdre took Kevin to visit. It had a huge variety of tropical and exotic birds—macaws, parrots, cockatoos and vultures, eagles, secretary birds and great bustards. Kevin was enthralled. "Awesome," he would sometimes say, when they stopped outside a birdcage. He especially loved an aviary with humming-birds that hovered around artificial flowers and sipped the nectar that they held.

Then, on another occasion, they visited a butterfly farm, where you could enter an enclosure, and the beautiful tropical butterflies would alight on your shoulder or a held out hand. Kevin liked the enclosed area that held a variety of different insects—like stick insects. There were also tarantulas in glass cases.

"Blimey!" he said. "You can imagine what Mum would say if I brought back one of these!"

Deirdre laughed. "Yes, she wouldn't be very pleased."

She even took him for a day trip in to London on the train and they visited the Natural History Museum. He was particularly impressed with the fossils of dinosaurs. "Awesome!" he exclaimed when he saw the fossils of Tyrannosaurus Rex and other huge monsters. "It's just like 'Jurassic Park'."

Deirdre felt she was on holiday herself. She had seldom gone out in all the years since Howard died. The use of her car was usually confined to trips to the village or Cambridge to shop. Now she was making full use of her little Renault Clio, and though her driving was erratic and she often lost her way, she liked driving in the countryside and enjoying the beautiful scenery.

Kevin suggested she buy a Tom Tom satellite navigation device.

"Good Heavens, Kevin," she said. "I would never be able to manage such a complicated gadget."

"It's easy," he said. "Don't worry, De-De, I'll work it for you."

So, it was a trip to Curry's in Cambridge, where she bought the device. It sat comfortably in a sort of pad on her dashboard, and wherever they wanted to go, Kevin would ask for the address or Post Code, and with a few taps of his dextrous fingers, he would program it, and it would take them wherever they wished until they reached their destination.

Deirdre took him to Stonehenge one day, but he was not very impressed, and though she tried to explain its history, he became bored and disinterested. "It's just a pile of rocks," he said. The same thing happened with one of the stately homes they visited. "When are we going to get out of this dump?" So, she confined these outings to places she thought would be more interesting for him — particularly ones with animals.

They usually made these trips on weekdays, as Sharon was home on weekends and could take charge of Kevin. Then he was back to the X-Box or laptop.

The school holidays came to an end — all too soon, as far as Deirdre was concerned, and it was back to school for Kevin. She would watch him and his mother leave the house in the morning, he with his backpack strapped to his back, and then they would return in the afternoon, when Sharon collected him from school and brought him home. So Deirdre was relieved of her baby-sitting — or, more appropriately, child minding responsibilities — at least during the daytime.

However, Sharon would often go down to the pub of an evening. On one such occasion, she asked Deirdre if she wouldn't mind helping Kevin with his bath.

"He can bathe himself," she said, "but sometimes I go in and scrub his back for him."

Deirdre filled the bathtub, careful to make sure the water was not too hot and, on Kevin's insistence, put in plenty of his bubble-bath and some of his toys, including the customary rubber-duck.

"Now, get undressed, Dear, and pop into the bath and give me a call if you need anything," Deirdre said.

She left Kevin in the bathroom and went downstairs for a cup of tea—or rather a drink! She heard him shout from the landing as she sipped her Scotch and water, watching the television.

"De-De. Come and do my back."

By the time she got up the stairs he was already back in the tub, and a puddle of water pooled where he had stood on the landing, and his wet footprints patterned the varnished wooden floor.

Steam filled the bathroom and the mirror was already fogged-up.

Kevin sat in the middle of the tub, with his back to the mixer tap, surrounded by foam, his toys floating around him.

"Shall I do your back with Sponge-whatever-his-name?" she said and gave him a wink.

"Oh, yeah," he said and handed her the dripping natural sponge. "It does look a bit like him."

He leaned forward and she started with the back of his neck, then worked her way down until he was covered in soap. She had never bathed a child in her lifetime and this was an entirely new experience for her.

"De-De, what's a cunt?" he suddenly said.

She was taken aback momentarily.

"Why do you ask, Dear?"

"One of the boys in school said I was a cunt."

Years of experience teaching schoolchildren about sex came to the fore, and she decided not to mince her words.

"Well, Kevin dear," she said. "It's a crude term for a girl's vagina. You know what a vagina is, don't you?"

"Yeah. It's a girl's pussy."

"That's also another crude term. Its proper name is vagina."

"And a boy. It's called a prick—right? I've been called that too."

"More correctly, it's penis, Dear,"

"Why don't they just call you a penis or vagina then?"

"Oh, people resort to these profanities when they want to abuse or insult you. The proper names of the male and female genitalia would not adequately fulfil their purpose."

"I suppose it's the same with fuck."

"Yes, Dear. The correct term is sexual intercourse."

"But you can't say 'you're a stupid sexual intercourse' can you?"

"No, I suppose you can't, Dear. It wouldn't be an insult then."

Kevin suddenly stood up in the tub, presenting Deirdre with a full view of his frontal nudity. It came as quite a shock to her. She couldn't remember ever seeing a fully naked child before. It was outside her experience. He looked like a pink peeled shrimp.

She averted her gaze and handed him the large bath towel from the rail.

"Now, dry yourself off, Dear, and I'll go downstairs and

make us a nice cup of hot cocoa. Then you can put on your night suit and dressing gown, and watch television for half-an-hour before bed."

"Really? That's awesome." Kevin surprised her then, when he reached up and gave her a quick hug.

Goodness, she thought as she stirred the cocoa powder into two hot mugs of milk, I'm really getting some experience in dealing with children—bathing and wiping bottoms and such. I used to deal only with their minds. Now it's coming to their bodies as well!

She thought about what Kevin had said, and smiled to herself. How different in her day when forbidden words were never uttered—at least never in the presence of adults. Previously, sex talk would be confined to the back of bicycle sheds, now it was so openly discussed in schools, and she had taken part in sex education sessions for the older children—discussing sexually transmitted diseases and birth control. She had even demonstrated how to cover an erect penis with a condom — using a model, of course. There had been giggles and sniggers, but she always dealt with their questions in a matter-of-fact way.

Deirdre sighed. There were so many young girls becoming pregnant at such a tender age, and she sometimes thought that perhaps too much knowledge about sex could be as dangerous as too little.

Kevin came downstairs and switched on the television. It was still before nine o'clock, so he was still within the parameters of his TV viewing. She took in the cocoa on a tray, accompanied by a plate of chocolate-chip biscuits.

"De-De," he said as she handed him his mug of hot cocoa. "Why didn't you have any kids?"

"Well, Dear," she said, "we never thought of starting a family — my husband and I, that is."

"Why not?"

"Oh I don't know. Perhaps Howard and I thought it would have been too much of a tie, and bringing up children is an awful responsibility."

He blew into his mug. "It's a pity," he said, "you would have made a great mum."

"Thank you, Kevin. That's a very kind thought. Don't you think you have a great mum too?"

"Yeah. But, I dunno. She gets on my back a lot. I miss not having a dad."

"Do you think it would have made a difference?"

"Yeah. All the other boys at school talk about their dads — at least a lot of them do. Those that have dads."

"Are there many who don't?"

"Yeah. Some kids have two dads, you know — or two mums, if their parents are queers."

"Ah. That's another derogatory term. More correctly they are known as gays."

"Yeah. But how do gays have sex?"

"That's another question you'll learn the answer to when you are older, Dear. For the moment let's just say that when two people love each other and are happy together, it does not really matter whether they are of the same sex or not."

"We have a boy who's queer—I mean, gay. Some of the other boys really take the piss ... err ... I mean, mickey out of him and call him a 'poofta'."

"Yes, it can be very hard for someone who is attracted to someone of the same sex, particularly in their early years. And, when someone is different, others—especially children, can be very cruel. It's really a lack of understanding on their part—or ignorance, to use a better word. Now, come on, Dear, and drink up your cocoa, it's nearing bedtime."

"Okay, De-De. Will you tuck me in and read to me again?"

"Of course I will, Dear. I'm beginning to quite enjoy the Harry Potter stories."

"Really? That's cool."

This time, after tucking him in bed and reading to him, she kissed him lightly on the forehead when she said 'goodnight'

Chapter 6

Sharon's nightly visits to the pub became more frequent, and Deirdre guessed she might be on the lookout for a boyfriend, since she apparently did not have one at present.

One day, as she was passing 'The Soldier of Fortune', Deirdre popped in for a quick drink.

"Hello, Deirdre girl," Bill, the publican, said from behind the bar. "Nice to see you after such a long while. What have you been doing with yourself?"

"Oh, I've been busy with this and that," Deirdre said.

"What'll you have? The usual?"

"Make it a gin and tonic, this time," Deirdre said, "It's simply too warm for Scotch."

"Ice and lemon?"

"Yes, plenty of it."

He dispensed a measure of spirit into a tumbler from the optic attached to a bottle of Gordon's, which hung upside down on the rack behind him.

Then he popped some lemon slices and ice-cubes into the glass and topped it up with tonic water.

"I hear you have a lodger now," he said.

"Yes, a young lady and her little boy."

"Two of them?"

"Yes, she's a single mother and was looking around for a place to stay and, as you know, I have a big house."

"That's really nice of you." Bill wiped the bar top with a sad looking cloth. "I guess she's the one who's here most evenings. The one with the streak in her hair and dangly earrings."

"That's an apt description. What does she usually drink?"

"Oh, vodka and lemonade or a Bacardi and Coke."

"Is she usually alone?" Deirdre asked, hoping it did not sound like prying.

"Yes, at first," Bill said. "Now she seems to have met someone and they sit at a table in the corner. He looks a bit of a weirdo."

"Ah! I thought she might have found someone. Do you

know him at all?"

"No, he's new. Never saw him before until she brought him in. Doesn't seem to be from the village."

"Well, here's cheers," Deirdre said and took a swig from her glass.

She stood at the bar with her drink while Bill busied himself with other customers. So, Sharon had found someone, she reflected. Well, good for her!

Sharon confirmed her friendship with her new boyfriend the following weekend, when she said, "Deirdre, I'll be taking Kev out today. I met this really cool guy one day, when he came into the flower shop. His name's Anton, and he has a car."

"Oh, I'm so pleased you've met someone, Dear," Deirdre said. "Has he met Kevin yet?"

"Naw. He didn't know about Kev until I mentioned it last evening. That's why we're going out together today so that they can get to know each other."

"Well, I'm sure you'll enjoy your day. It's lovely and

sunny. Are you going into the country?"

"Just to Royston where he lives — about fifteen miles from here."

"Does he have a house there?"

"He lives with his mum. But we won't be going to his place. Just to a park in the town. We plan to have a picnic there."

"That's nice, Dear. You have a lovely time."

Anton called round about an hour or so later in his car. It was an old VW combi, painted purple and decorated with flower designs — a remnant of the hippy days. He parked outside the gate, and through the front window, Deirdre caught a glimpse of him as he sat behind the steering wheel. She saw Sharon, with Kevin in tow, exit the front door carrying a cool box between them. She did not see anything more of the boyfriend, as he did not get out of the car to open the doors for them. They drove off in a billow of black smoke spewing from the car's noisy exhaust.

The next day, as Deirdre and Kevin knelt beside the pond trying to find the newt, she asked him, "How did you get on with your mum's new boyfriend yesterday?"

"Who, Anton? He's a real weirdo."

"What makes you say that, Dear?"

"Dunno. It's just the things he says and does. He's weird."

"In what way?"

"Well, I think he's into Hinduism or something. He keeps talking about a thing called korma."

"I think you may mean karma, Dear."

"What's that?"

"Well, it's a philosophy that believes that when you pass on from this world, you come back to earth in another incarnation — that is, you live several lives, and your fate is determined by your karma — how well, or how badly you lived your previous life."

"You mean like Doctor Who? He comes back in these different carnation things if he gets killed or injured in some way as he travels through time."

"I don't think it's quite the same thing, Dear. And look, I think we've found your newt."

"Oh yeah — there he is. That's awesome!"

"Have you thought of a name for him yet?"

"Yeah, I think I'll call him Isaac."

"Why Isaac?"

"Well, you know, Isaac Newton. 'Newt — on'," he emphasised. "You get it?"

"Ah, yes, I do. The famous astronomer. That's clever!"

That was all Deirdre was going to learn about Anton from Kevin for that day. But, a few days later, Deirdre actually met Anton when he dropped Sharon back home from work. Sharon invited him into the house and introduced him to Deirdre.

"Hi Deirdre," she said. "This is my new friend Anton."

Deirdre could now understand why Bill — and Kevin for that matter — had described him as a weirdo. He had a young face, with a slight growth of beard, and his fair hair plaited into rat's tails that hung from his head in strands. He wore a sort of tunic and around his neck hung a necklace of large beads, much like the sadhus of India wear. He gave Deirdre's hand a limp shake.

Then Sharon handed Deirdre a large bunch of flowers. "And these are from Anton and me, for all your kindness."

Deirdre was touched, and more than a little surprised. "How very nice of you both. Now, you two go into the front room and make yourselves comfortable while I find a vase to put these in. A cup of tea for both of you?"

"Coffee," they said in unison. "No milk for Anton," Sharon added.

"Of course. Where is Kevin?"

"Oh, he's been kept back in school for detention. Anton will pick him up later."

"Oh dear, what did he do?"

"He used a swearword at one of the boys in class and the teacher overheard."

"Oh dear." Deirdre wondered whether it was one of the words he'd asked her about while he was having his bath. It probably was.

A few nights later, when she was reading in bed, Deirdre heard Sharon and Anton creep into the house from an evening out. Their footsteps trod up the stairs and it was obvious there were more than one pair. Whispers and giggles also drifted into her room, and the door to Sharon's bedroom opened then closed again. Ah. It's happened, Deirdre thought—overnight visitors. She had felt it would happen at some point. The young lived very much more active sexual lives today than in Deirdre's day.

Sometime later, Deirdre got up to use the toilet, and could hear low moans, panting, and the rhythmic squeaking of the bed, coming from the room. Sex had raised its ugly head.

Anton left before Deirdre got out of bed in the morning. She heard hushed voices again, and footsteps down the stairs. Then she heard his car engine start, and the car driving off.

She voiced her concerns to Mildred the next day, on the

telephone.

"Well, it depends on how you feel about this, Deirdre," Mildred said. "Many landlords or landladies these days don't object to overnight visitors. But, it's your prerogative. You set the rules, because after all, it is your home. Did you make this clear to her before you let it out?"

"I can't for the life or me remember whether I did or didn't."

"Well then, you have two choices," Mildred said. "You can either turn a blind eye or confront her about it."

"Oh dear," Deirdre said. She hated confrontation of any kind, being a bit of a moral coward in this regard. 'Peace at any price' was her motto, and she usually shied away from arguments or political debate.

"I think I'll just let it go, Mildred dear. It wouldn't be fair if I hadn't made it clear about overnight guests at the outset." However, Deirdre still felt uncomfortable about the situation, especially with an impressionable child, like Kevin, around. So she welcomed Mildred's sensible advice.

The friendship between Sharon and Anton seemed to develop over the course of the next month or so, and they would sometimes be away over the weekend. They usually left Kevin behind in Deirdre's care on these occasions, but Sharon would always ask Deirdre if she minded, and would appear grateful when she acquiesced.

Deirdre minded less and less looking after Kevin. She enjoyed his lively chatter and even his mischief sometimes, like the day he was helping Deirdre do a bit of light gardening. Deirdre usually employed 'dear Mr Fowler' who kept the garden up to scratch, doing all the heavy work. As she worked, planting a few plants, she noticed Kevin standing with his back towards her over a flowerbed. His attitude suggested he was doing a wee.

"Kevin. What on earth are you doing, Dear?" she said.

"Just giving the marigolds a bit of water, De-De," he said. He glanced over his shoulder, and his grin looked wicked.

"Oh dear," Deirdre said. "Please don't, Kevin dear. Don't

water the marigolds that way."

"It's good for them," he said, "after all, you use horse shit as manure, so what's the harm in a little bit of piss?"

She noticed his language had become more and more crude as the days went by. At first he watched his tongue, but as he got more familiar with Deirdre he was less careful about his language.

Unsure whether it was the right choice or not, Deirdre decided to keep quiet about it for the time being. She felt sure that Kevin did not really have any other adult in his life he could relate to, the way he did with her. Besides, words, like the F-word, were used so regularly in films and TV programmes that she had become quite immune to them.

"I'm sure it won't do them any harm, but there's a perfectly good watering can in the shed," she said. "So, if you need to water the plants, please use that, Dear."

"Okey-dokey," Kevin said and did up his flies. "Whatever you say."

Then, on another day, she heard Kevin shouting out from the landing, "De-De, there's a great big fucking spider in the tub."

"Hang on, Dear," she called out. "Don't harm it."

She had dealt with spiders trapped in the bath before. She went into the kitchen and got out a small glass bowl from the cabinet, then retrieved a coaster from the living room.

True enough, the spider was in the bathtub, trying desperately to crawl out but falling back into the tub each time its feet lost their grip on the sides.

"Now, Dear," she said, "I'm going to place the bowl over the spider, then gently slide the coaster underneath. Then we can take it out of the tub."

"Let me do it." Kevin pleaded as much with his eyes as with his words.

"All right, but be careful, especially when you slide the coaster underneath. We don't want to trap its legs."

The task accomplished, Kevin held up the coaster and glass bowl containing the spider, which tried frenziedly to escape its confinement. "Gosh! It's awesome," he said.

They took it out of the house and into the garden.

"Now, " Deirdre said, "just put it all down on the pathway and then lift the bowl off quickly."

Kevin did as instructed, and the spider made a bid for freedom, scuttling off into the grass verge.

"I guess he'll be okay," Kevin said.

"I'm sure he will, Dear. He'll find plenty of little flies to eat."

"Mum would have killed it," Kevin said. "She's terrified of spiders. You're not, are you, De-De?"

"No," she said, "They're all nature's little creatures, and then, of course, I do believe in karma."

"You mean the carnation thing?"

"Reincarnation, Dear. It is a Buddhist and Hindu philosophy that we have all lived past lives, sometimes as little creatures, like the spider. Then, when that life ends, we are reincarnated into some other living creature, and so we progress up the scale until we perhaps become a human being."

"What happens then?"

"Well," Deirdre explained. "If one's karma is good, we return in another incarnation and live a better life — in fact, perhaps several such lives, until we reach a state of Nirvana."

"What's that?"

"It means a blissful state of perfect peace and tranquillity."

"You don't believe in God and Heaven, then?"

"Well, I do in a way," Deirdre said. "But I have a different concept of God and Heaven."

"I don't believe in God or Heaven," Kevin said.

"Well, Dear, it depends very much on the way you were brought up. My mother and father, for instance, were not very devout Christians, and as a little girl, they allowed me to form my own beliefs. Howard, on the other hand, had a strict religious upbringing, but as he grew up and developed an interest in science and astronomy, his religious conviction became less and less."

"I like astronomy," Kevin said, "the stars and things."

"Well then, the next clear night we will have to go out in the back garden and have a look at the sky. I think Howard's old telescope is still somewhere in the loft."

"That's cool," Kevin said. "We will do that one night, won't we, De-De? Promise?"

"Of course we shall."

With the promise duly made, they went back into the house.

Chapter 7

Sharon and Anton's relationship progressed over the weeks. They were away most weekends and left Deirdre to take care of Kevin. When Deirdre approached Sharon about this, Sharon said, "Kev and Anton don't get on too well."

"Why is that, Dear?"

"Well, Anton doesn't like kids very much," Sharon said, "and Kev would be in the way. "You see," she continued, "Anton didn't know about Kev until I told him." The young woman avoided Deirdre's gaze.

"I see," Deirdre said. She felt uncomfortable with this conversation.

"He didn't know that I was a single mum when I first met him, and it came as a bit of a shock. In fact, he thought I was younger than I really am."

"I don't mean to pry," Deirdre said, "but who was Kevin's father?"

"Oh, he was just a guy I met when I was sixteen. He made me pregnant. I wasn't on the pill or anything, and he didn't use a condom, so the result was Kev." Sharon picked at a bit of fluff on the chair arm.

"I see, Dear. It must have been very difficult for you, at that young age."

"Yeah," Sharon said. "It was really tough. I don't think Kev likes Anton very much either. You see," she continued, "Anton doesn't get on with kids. He says they're always in the way and too much of a pain."

When Deirdre asked Kevin's opinion of Anton, his reaction was, "He's such a weirdo. He won't eat meat or anything. He won't even let me have a McDonald's burger."

"He's probably a vegan," Deirdre said.

"What's that?"

"Someone who doesn't eat animal products like meat or eggs," Deirdre said. "You mentioned that he was into Hinduism. Well, most Hindus — at least those of a higher caste—are mostly vegetarians."

"Yeah, he's a real weirdo. And, he's got Mum on to it too. She won't eat meat now."

"Oh dear," Deirdre said, "and here I was planning on cooking a roast lamb dinner for all of you. Good thing you warned me."

"But you'll make it for me, won't you, De-De? I haven't had roast lamb for ages."

"Of course I will, Dear. Perhaps one weekend when they're away." She couldn't help but ruffle his hair. Deirdre had become quite fond of the boy.

Not only did the weekends away continue, but also one week, Sharon didn't return home at all. Deirdre felt concerned and rang the flower shop where Sharon worked. She was told that Sharon hadn't been in to work all week.

When she asked Kevin about this he said, "She's done this before. Left me with friends while she went off with some bloke."

The week turned into two, and Deirdre had a call from the flower shop saying that they were terminating Sharon's employment. She immediately rang Mildred.

"She is still receiving her benefit," Mildred said. "But, if she has made herself unemployed, it will complicate things and she may lose her entitlement."

"I'm more concerned about Kevin," Deirdre said. "The poor child seems to have been abandoned and foisted on to me."

"I can sympathise with your predicament," Mildred said. "Perhaps we should take him into care."

"Oh dear," Deirdre said. "That would be rather drastic. I don't mind taking care of Kevin, you know. He's no trouble, and he seems to be happy with me."

"Well, we know he is in good hands. There's no one more responsible than you are. It is you that I am concerned about."

"Oh, I'm all right. I think I can cope with Kevin. I'm beginning to get quite fond of him, you know."

"We shall leave things as they stand at the present then," Mildred said. "But if the situation changes or any further problems develop, please let me know."

In truth, Deirdre did not mind having Kevin to herself as the weeks went by. She actually enjoyed the new responsibility imposed upon her, getting him up in the morning; seeing he was ready for school on time; giving him his breakfast—usually a bowl of Coco Pops and a glass of milk; packing his lunch-box with a sandwich and an apple or banana; taking him to school, and collecting him in the afternoon.

In the evening, after watching his favourite TV programs, she would help him with his homework at the kitchen table. Then it was the nightly ritual of putting him to bed, tucking him in and reading to him from his Harry Potter book. Now, she always gave him a kiss on the forehead before she left his room.

The only problem was at suppertime. Deirdre tried her best to change his usual diet to a healthier one, but Kevin resisted her efforts at first. However, she persevered and gradually introduced new appetising and healthy meals, which he eventually ate without a fuss.

On weekends, they would go out on day-trips. One day, she took him to a farm, where her farmer-friend showed him around. He was enthralled at the cows and pigs, and the snorting bull in his pen. "Awesome" would be his usual remark.

Then, one fine night, they went into the back garden to look at the stars. Kevin had retrieved Howard's telescope from the loft where it had been gathering dust. It was a Newtonian reflecting telescope with a six-inch mirror. A good pair of binoculars also hung in the hallway.

Deirdre explained the constellations to Kevin.

"Now, Dear, you see that pattern of stars in the sky that looks like a big 'W'? Well, that's Cassiopeia and the bright star further down is the Pole Star. Then we come to the Great Bear or Big Dipper, as the Americans call it. It looks like a pan with a handle."

When it came to finding a star and focussing on it through the telescope, Deirdre explained, "You see that star over there? It looks like one star, but then if you look at it through the telescope, you will find there are really two stars in close orbit around each other."

"Yeah," Kevin said. "Awesome."

She pointed out the planet Jupiter, and when Kevin found it in the telescope, Deirdre said, "Now look hard, Kevin dear, and you'll see some tiny pinpoints of light around it. Those are the four Galilean moons that orbit their mother planet."

"Oh yeah, I see them — cool."

"We'll come out another night when the Moon is out," Deirdre said. "And then you'll be able to see all the craters on it."

All this while, there had been no word from Sharon, not even a telephone call. "I feel she has really abandoned him," Deirdre told Mildred on the phone. "Do you have any idea where she may be?"

"We have heard nothing. However, she is not claiming her benefit now. That is all we know."

"Perhaps they've gone off somewhere—Europe or even India. Kevin says that her boyfriend is into Hinduism, so it wouldn't be surprising."

"Well, we will soon have to make some decision about Kevin's future. Have you considered fostering him?"

"Not really. Do you think it will have to come to that?"

"It may well do. We cannot just leave him in limbo."

"Well, whatever you think best. Would it be a problem, my fostering him?"

"Deirdre, we have known you all these years and probably could not find someone more responsible or suitable to care for him."

"I'm not sure what formalities will have to be gone through. Would I be acceptable as a foster parent, taking my age into consideration?"

"I am sure you will qualify quite easily. Age is not a problem, providing you are fit and healthy. Of course there will be forms to be filled and all the formalities will have to be gone through, but I am sure in the end there will be no problem placing Kevin in your care."

"Can I see you about it, Mildred dear?"

"Certainly. Look, I will come over to your place and bring over some forms and leaflets on fostering. We can discuss it in detail over a cup of tea. But, are you sure you are not taking on too much?"

"I think I'm quite clear in my mind, Dear. I wouldn't like Kevin to be placed in care, if my fostering is an alternative."

"That is settled then," Mildred said. A mutual date was set for a visit, and Deirdre put down the phone. But, of course, she had to speak to Kevin about the plan.

She broached the subject after school, while Kevin ate his tea.

"We don't know where your mum is, Kevin dear. There has been no news from her for several weeks now."

He shrugged and stared at his plate. "Mum's always like that when she gets a boyfriend—like a bitch on heat."

"Kevin! If you mean to shock me, you have succeeded," she said. "Where on earth do you learn such phrases?"

"In school."

"You wouldn't mind living here, with an old lady like me?"

"I love you, De-De," he said. "It'll be really cool living with you."

Deirdre was touched by his words. "And I love you too, Dear." She reached across the table and took his hand. He picked it up and placed it to his lips and kissed it.

Chapter 8

Kevin's tenth birthday was fast approaching, and Deirdre began to make plans for it. She wanted to give him a bicycle, but had no idea what kind, so she rang her friend Dave, for suggestions.

"My little nipper has a BMX model and he's in love with it," Dave said. "It's a bit expensive, but it's good quality and value for money."

"Would you do a great favour for me, Dear, and help choose one for me?"

"I will indeed. Would you like me to come around to your place and pick you up? Then I can take you to the cycle shop in Cambridge."

"That is extremely kind of you, Dear."

"When is Kevin's birthday?"

"It's on Saturday week."

Deirdre decided she would have a party for Kevin in the

back garden. She discussed her plans with Kevin that evening.

"You're having a party for me? That's cool. I've never had a real birthday party before. Thank you, De-De." He gave her a big hug, and squeezed tight, even though his arms didn't' reach much past her sides.

"Now, Dear, make a list of the friends you would like to invite, so that I know how many there will be. I would like to ask my friend Dave, his wife and their young son, and also a few of my other friends, if that's all right?"

"Yeah, sure," Kevin said. "Whatever."

As promised, Dave came round a few days later in his van and picked Deirdre up. He took her to the 'Cyclopedia' shop in Cambridge, where they had a fine selection of children's bicycles. Dave helped her choose a suitable model, plus a helmet. Then Dave brought Deirdre back home and they hid the bicycle in the garage behind some cardboard boxes, so that Kevin would not see it.

Deirdre then formulated her plans for the party. Again, this was an entirely new experience for her. Of course, she had attended children's parties before, so she had some ideas of what was required.

She would definitely include Mildred and a couple more of her older friends. When she went into neighbouring Cambridge, she ordered a birthday cake at the bakers, and went shopping for birthday candles, party hats, balloons, and other paraphernalia. Then she went to the Marks food-store and did the necessary shopping for the party food. She also decided to hire a magician to keep the children amused, and looked through Yellow Pages for someone suitable.

Deirdre wondered whether Sharon would remember her child's birthday and send him a birthday card. One did arrive through the letterbox, but it took the form of a postcard of an Ashram in India. On the back, Sharon had scrawled, "Happy Birthday, Kev—Mum and Anton." Below was a PS—"Tell Deirdre I'm sorry and that I'll be writing." This confirmed Deirdre's suspicions that Sharon and Anton had indeed left the country and gone to India, probably as back-packers. They were obviously living in the Ashram pictured on the card, in Kolkata — or Calcutta, as it was previously known.

Deirdre was familiar with India, and indeed Calcutta. In fact, she had been born there and spent part of her childhood in the hills of Darjeeling, where she had gone to boarding school. Then, with the fading of the influence of the British Raj after Indian independence, her parents had brought her to England.

The day of Kevin's birthday arrived. When he came into the kitchen, still in his pyjamas, she greeted him with "Happy Birthday, Kevin, dear." And gave him a big hug. "Now, after your breakfast, I have a surprise for you."

Kevin gobbled up his Coco Pops and milk at lightning speed. "Where is it, De-De?" He wriggled on the chair in his excitement.

"It's in the garage. Go upstairs and get dressed, Dear, then I'll show it to you."

Kevin did as bid and, when he came downstairs again, Deirdre led him to the garage. The brand-new shiny bicycle was revealed to him in all its glory. Deirdre had taken it out of its hiding place and placed it on its stand beside her car. She had tied floating foil balloons to the handlebars with 'Happy Birthday' written on them. Satin ribbons, tied in bows, festooned the bike.

"Gosh! Awesome," Kevin said, as he hugged her. "Kiss," he demanded.

She bent down and he plastered her with feverish kisses on both cheeks. "I really love you, De-De."

Once she had recovered her composure, she gave him a cuddle, then asked, "Do you know how to ride a bicycle?" She couldn't remember when a child had last kissed her.

"Yeah. I learned on a friend's."

"Good," she said. "Now we can go for rides in the country." She had an ancient Rudge, with a basket attached to the handlebars.

Later in the morning, Kevin helped her extract a long trellis table from the garage and two wooden benches. They took these to the back garden, and Deirdre decorated the surrounding area with bunting and streamers. She got Kevin to blow up the balloons, and when they had finished everything looked gay and festive, with paper-hats, blowouts and a little gift parcel for each of his friends at every place setting.

Deirdre busied herself in the kitchen, preparing all the party food. There were cup-cakes, jellies, sandwiches, sausage-rolls and other treats and goodies, and of course, Kevin's birthday cake, adorned with ten candles.

At about four in the afternoon, the first guests arrived. Each of Kevin's school friends carried a birthday gift, which they handed to him. Dave's little boy also brought him a gift, and his parents too.

"Gosh," he said to Deirdre, "I've never had so many presents on my birthday before."

Seated at the table, the children scoffed their food, then the magician arrived to entertain them with his magic tricks, while the grown-ups, including Mildred, sat in the conservatory to get away from all the hustle and bustle. Deirdre served them tea from her silver tea service, with plates of dainty sandwiches and teacakes.

All in all, it had been a great success, Deirdre thought as she went to bed, utterly exhausted by the day's events. However, it had been a completely rewarding experience for her. Of course, there were a few incidents, like one little girl getting sick after eating too many sweets and cakes, and then there was a bit of argy-bargy between two little boys, squabbling over some toy or other.

Pleasure filled the days that followed. Deirdre and Kevin went for rides in the country, she astride her ancient Rudge, and he, wearing his helmet, on his brand-new bicycle. On these occasions, Deirdre would pack a picnic basket, and they would sit under an apple tree in the farmer's orchard and enjoy the peace and tranquillity, broken only by the singing of birds. Sometimes, she would take Howard's binoculars, and they would do a bit of bird-watching.

Then, one afternoon, while Deirdre sat in her armchair crocheting a tablemat, the doorbell rang. She went to the front door and opened it, and there, on the threshold, stood Sharon.

"I've come for Kev," she said.

Chapter 9

"My goodness!" Deirdre exclaimed. "Where on earth have you been all this while?"

"I've just come back from India, with Anton," Sharon said. "Didn't you get my letter?"

"No, I didn't. All we had was a post-card from you for Kevin's birthday. It did indicate that you were in India."

"Yeah," Sharon said. "Anton and I got married there. We had a Hindu wedding, because we've both converted to Hinduism while we were there."

Deirdre noticed that Sharon, in addition to her face decorations, now sported a red *tikka* in the middle of her forehead, indicating a married Indian woman.

"But why in heaven's name didn't you tell us you were going away? We have been frantic with worry about you, especially Kevin," she lied.

"Well, I couldn't." She spoke in a slow drawl, and looked as though she didn't care. "We made our plans in a hurry.

We couldn't take Kev with us, and I felt too afraid to ask you to look after him while we were away, in case you refused."

"That was extremely naughty of you," Deirdre said. "Of course I would have taken care of Kevin whilst you were away, if only you had asked."

"I couldn't take the chance," Sharon said. "Anyway," she continued, "we're married now and would like to have Kev back. Where is he?"

"He's still at school, but it's soon time for him to come home. I thought Anton didn't want to be burdened with children."

"Yeah, at first he didn't," Sharon said, "but after being in India and getting married and all, he's reconsidered. I'll tell Anton to go fetch him from school. He's waiting outside in the combi."

"I don't think that will be necessary. Kevin has a bicycle now and goes to school on it by himself."

"He has a bike now? Who gave it to him?"

"I did, as a matter of fact," Deirdre said. "For his birthday."

Sharon either missed or ignored the crisp tone. "That was nice of you. He's never had a bike before."

Deirdre was heartily sick of Sharon's drawl. "And what about your room?" Deirdre asked. "I suppose you don't require it anymore."

"Yeah, I realise that I owe you for the rent, but that's okay. Anton has some money left, even though our trip nearly broke the bank. We worked it out and here's a cheque to square up with you." She handed the cheque over. "Thanks for waiting. I'll pack up the rest of my things. I don't have much, only some clothes and shoes, and some of my cosmetics."

"Well, I was more concerned about Kevin," Deirdre said. "He felt completely abandoned by you."

"Oh, Kev's all right. I've left him with friends before now."

Oblivious to Deirdre's disapproval, Sharon went upstairs and packed up her things, and when she came down again she had a suitcase and a couple of carrier bags.

Kevin arrived back from school a short while later.

Deirdre watched through the window as he put his bicycle away carefully in the garage and came into the house. He was not completely surprised by his mother's unexpected return, as he had spotted Anton's combi parked outside the gate.

"Kev!" Sharon exclaimed, opening her arms wide. "Mummy's been a naughty girl, but she's back now to take care of you."

Kevin went up to her and pecked her coldly on the cheek when she embraced him.

"Mum and Anton are married now," she declared. "So you have a new dad, and we've come to take you home. Go get your things, and take them to the car."

"I'm not going," Kevin said and a stubborn look settled onto his face. He looked at Deirdre. "Can't I stay here?" His bottom lip trembled.

"I'm afraid not, Kevin dear," Deirdre said, as gently as possible. "You'll have to go with your mother. So, be a good boy and get your things, as your mother says."

"It'll take me time to pack up all my stuff. Can't you come back for me?"

"No," Sharon said. "Anton and I'll wait. There's no hurry."

While he was gone, Sharon told Deirdre all about her experiences in India, her conversion to Hinduism and what a fabulous guy Anton was. Deirdre listened with a pensive finger to her cheek, and just gave a "um-hum," in response at appropriate moments. She was still reeling from shock at Sharon's unexpected return. She had no control over events. Sharon was Kevin's mother and Deirdre had no legal rights over him whatsoever, and that was that.

Sharon said she was desperate for a fag, so Deirdre told her she could go into the conservatory and have a cigarette there. While she was gone, Deirdre poured herself a stiff whiskey from the cabinet. She really needed one. Meanwhile, Kevin made trips up and down the stairs, carrying his possessions in cardboard boxes, to the combi where Anton waited.

The dreaded moment arrived and it was time to say goodbye. Kevin hugged Deirdre around her middle. He had grown over the past few months, and his arms reached a good deal further around her waist by now. "Goodbye, De-De," he said. "Can I come and see you sometimes?"

"That's if Deirdre will have you," Sharon said. "She must be pretty fed-up with you by now."

"Of course you can, Dear. I will be most pleased to see you."

"And you'll look after Isaac for me?" Kevin said.

"Indeed I will. Now, don't forget your bicycle."

"Oh, yeah. Can't I leave it here for when I come to see you?"

"Of course you may, if you wish," Deirdre said.

"You can stay with Deirdre on a weekend if you like," Sharon said, "provided she doesn't mind and you behave yourself and don't become a nuisance."

"Kevin will be a most welcome guest," Deirdre said. "We have become very good friends."

"Bye bye, De-De," Kevin said, hugging her again. His eyes brimmed with tears. "I'm going to miss you."

"And I'm going to miss you too, Dear."

"And bye-bye, Timothy," Kevin said, stroking Timothy's head. "I guess I'll miss you too."

"Cheer up, Kev," Sharon said. "You've got a new dad now. Something you've always wanted. Aren't you excited about that?"

Kevin shrugged. "Yeah, I suppose."

"Well, ta-ra, Deirdre, and thank you for looking after Kev for Anton and me. I am sorry about everything, but I'm sure you understand."

With that, they left.

Chapter 10

Days filled with emptiness, passed slowly, following Kevin's departure. The old house seemed too large and quiet, and if it were not for Timothy's company, Deirdre would have felt lonelier still. What she wouldn't give to hear Kevin's chatter, his noisy computer games, and to have the bedtime ritual of tucking him in at night. She had thoroughly enjoyed looking after him and seeing to his needs. Her life now seemed empty and purposeless. She rang her friend Mildred, and told her of the events, and how much she missed not having Kevin around.

"You have become too emotionally attached to him," Mildred said with her usual practicality. "This so often happens when we have to remove a child from foster-care and return them to their natural parents."

"I know, Dear," Deirdre said. "I'm a silly old fool."

"No, Deirdre. You are simply a kind, generous and warm-hearted person who puts the welfare of others before yourself."

"Yes, that may be true to a point, but it has been a selfish life too, because not having any children, Howard and I had no one to think of besides ourselves."

"Yes, and of course, as a consequence, you do not have grandchildren either, which is a comfort in old age."

"Do you know, Dear," Deirdre confided, "I have never felt very close to anyone beside dear Howard and my parents throughout my entire life? Kevin seems to have been the first one to whom I have become so attached. I must admit, parting from him has been a terrible wrench."

"I understand. Try not to become too depressed or upset over the situation. Perhaps you will not lose contact with Kevin entirely, because he seems to have formed a bond with you."

"Yes, he did say he would like to visit me on occasion, and his mother agreed that he could sometimes spend a weekend with me."

"Well, there you are then. That will give you something to

look forward to."

Deirdre did not have too long to wait. The phone rang one afternoon and it was Kevin.

"De-De," he said, with the excitement evident in his voice, "Mum's agreed to let me spend next weekend with you. She and Anton are going off somewhere for the bank holiday, so he says he'll take me to you, and I can spend Friday, Saturday and Sunday night."

"Oh, I am so pleased," Deirdre said, "I have missed you so much and it would be so splendid to see you again."

"I've missed you too. Can we go for another bike ride into the country?"

"Of course we shall, Dear."

"How are Timothy and Isaac?"

"They're both fine. Timothy misses you too, and I saw Isaac the other day, swimming around in the pond. The little frog has come back too, and sits on the lily pad. I think he and Isaac have become friends."

"Awesome," Kevin said. "Love you, De-De."

"And I love you too, Kevin dear."

The days could not have passed quickly enough for Deirdre, as she made plans and preparations for Kevin's visit. Then, on the Friday evening, she heard Anton's combi screech to a halt outside her gate, the door slam and the combi race off again. Kevin appeared breathlessly at the front door, carrying an overnight bag. He hugged her as she met him. "I'm so happy, De-De," he said. "I thought I'd never see you again."

As they sat at the kitchen table, Kevin munching on a jam-and-peanut-butter sandwich, one of his favourite foods, he told Deirdre all about Anton and Sharon's relationship.

"He's such a weirdo," Kevin said. "He and mum are into this Kama Sutra thing — it's all about sex, you know."

"And how do you know that, Dear?"

"Well, he had this open book on their bed and one day I had a look at it. There were pictures of people having sex in all sorts of funny positions. It was really disgusting."

"Yes, Dear, I have heard about Kama Sutra. It's a very ancient Indian book about lovemaking."

"Yeah. And they're at it all night. I can hear them, and it's really sickening."

"Of course, Kevin, dear, lovemaking between married couples is a perfectly natural thing."

"Yeah, I guess. It's still disgusting. Now Mum says she's going to have another baby. She says it'll be a little brother or sister for me. Ugh."

"And how are you getting on with your new father?"

"Anton? He's not like a dad—not a real dad anyway. He just gets on my back and tries to boss me around. He called me a little bastard the other day—of course, not in front of Mum."

"Oh dear," Deirdre said.

"And then he and Mum are into this puja thing. They have their weirdo friends over of an evening, and they sit on the floor in a circle and clash cymbals together and chant words like 'Ram, Ram Sita Ram' and mumble weird prayers he calls mantras. Then they light candles and burn some sort of sticks that give off a funny smell."

"That's incense, Dear—joss sticks, they're called."

"Yeah. It smells sweet and horrible. Then," he continued with a scowl, "they won't eat meat—only vegetables made into some sort of curry, and then they eat a thing called dhal, which is terrible. It makes me want to puke."

"Those are lentils, Dear. They're very nourishing."

"They're disgusting! I managed to sneak in a hamburger that I bought from McDonald's with my lunch money, and Anton told me off and said I smelt of meat. Now they want me to become a Hindu like them." He clenched his fist on the tabletop. "I don't want to be a fucking Hindu."

"I'm sure you don't, Dear."

"It's all Anton's fault—all this Hindu stuff I mean, and my stupid Mum has become hooked on it."

"Well, Hinduism is a very ancient philosophy. It's very prevalent in India, and its customs and rituals may seem very strange to you."

"You don't believe in all this stupid stuff, do you?"

"Well, I do accept some of the Hindu and Buddhist philosophies—like reincarnation. But, of course, I'm not a practicing Hindu."

After supper, which consisted of Kentucky Fried Chicken and fries, which Deirdre had bought earlier from the KFC shop in Cambridge, they watched television, Kevin sitting on the sofa with Timothy on his lap. She indulged Kevin and let him watch his favourite programs, like 'Doctor Who'. This was followed by one of the Harry Potter films on one of the satellite channels.

"You can stay up till after nine o'clock, Kevin dear," Deirdre said, "as a special treat, seeing you're on holiday."

"Oh, cool," Kevin said. "Can we watch 'Terminator 2'? It's on after the news."

"As long as it's not too violent, Dear," Deirdre said.

"But I love violence," Kevin said, "and I've seen it before. And it's just violence—no sex or anything."

"Very well," Deirdre said with a sigh. "If you've seen it before, it can't do any harm."

He fell fast asleep before the end of the film, so Deirdre had to wake him up and take him upstairs to bed. She helped him undress and tucked him in. He was too sleepy for a story, so she kissed him on the forehead as she bid him goodnight.

Chapter 11

The next day dawned bright and sunny. An Indian summer bathed the country in late heat, so the weather remained warm, and it was an ideal day for a picnic. Deirdre packed a lunch basket with ham sandwiches, sausage rolls and an apple, for each of them. She made a thermos of tea for herself, and added a can of Coke for Kevin.

They wheeled their cycles out of the garage and rode along country lanes, until they reached their favourite picnic spot beneath the apple tree. Butterflies floated past and settled on wild-flowers, and bumblebees droned by lazily.

Deirdre poured herself some tea from the thermos, while Kevin munched on a ham sandwich and washed it down with a swig of Coke.

"It's great to have meat again," Kevin said. "This vegan thing is a real pain. How can people live on just vegetables?"

"Well, some people consider that killing animals for food is wrong," Deirdre said, "and that seems to be the principal reason for vegetarianism. I would become vegetarian too if it meant killing a chicken myself simply to eat it. It's only because it's all done for one that I can come to terms with eating meat."

"Yeah, I suppose. I wouldn't like killing anything either. Why do these Hindus have this thing about not eating meat?"

"Well, Dear, it's built into their religion by the caste system. Some Hindus *are* allowed to eat meat. It simply depends on how high up or low down you are on the caste structure. The high-caste Brahmins, for example, won't eat any animal produce, whereas the low-caste Harijans can eat virtually anything."

"Why's that?"

"Well, Dear, consider. If no one in India would have anything to do with handling animal products, who would do the menial jobs like tanning animal hides?"

"Yeah, I see. But why do they want to go about naked?"

"Do they? I don't know about that."

"Yeah. Anton walks about naked in the house. He has a

huge willy."

"Penis, Dear," Deirdre said. "But I don't know that walking around naked in the house is a Hindu custom. Of course, there are some holy men in India who wander about completely naked. They're called Sadhus."

"Yeah. But he does. Sometimes, Mum walks about naked too. They wanted me to, but I refused. I don't want anyone to see my willy—penis, I mean, especially not Anton."

"That's perfectly understandable, Dear. One has to preserve one's modesty."

"Maybe it's just because he's a weirdo."

"That would explain a lot," Deirdre said. "Now, finish the sandwiches and we'll make our way home."

In the evening, as they sat in the living room watching television, Deirdre asked Kevin what he would like for his supper.

"Can we just order a pizza, De-De, and eat it while we watch TV?"

"Of course we may," she said.

Although Deirdre had tried to coax Kevin into eating healthy food, he often got his way when it came to junk-food. He had introduced her to fast-food like Kentucky Fried Chicken, McDonald's burgers, and Pizzas, and she found them surprisingly tasty and quite delicious. It was no wonder that children ate them so eagerly, in preference to what was considered a healthy diet. It was ironical that all food that was supposed to be bad for you tasted so good! She remembered all the tasty snacks she ate in India as a child from roadside eating shops.

They ordered a pepperoni pizza from Dominos.

"Mum and Anton never order pizzas or anything," Kevin said. "She used to before, but not anymore."

"Is she working now?" Deirdre asked.

"Uh-huh. She has a job in some sort of fashion shop in the town, where they sell trendy stuff."

"And Anton?"

"He works as a delivery man, delivering stuff in a van."

"Oh well, at least they are both working. Do they live in a flat or in a house?"

"A flat," Kevin said. "It's a real dump."

"Anton used to live with his mother. Does she live close-by?"

"Yeah. They visit her sometimes and took me once to see her. She's a mean old bitch!"

A while later the pizza man arrived on his scooter and delivered the pizza. Deirdre took it into the kitchen and separated the slices. She put the pieces onto two dinner plates, which she then placed on trays. She took a can of Coke from the fridge and put it on Kevin's tray, and took it in to him. He lay on the floor, his eyes glued to the television. She placed the tray beside him.

"Thank you." His eyes never left the screen.

Deirdre returned to the kitchen and brought in her own tray, which held a glass of water with two lemon slices in it. A gin and tonic, or even a lager, would have been more welcome, she thought. But she didn't want to drink in front of the boy.

"They don't even have a television," Kevin complained, biting into his slice of pizza. "Anton has this thing about television. He says it corrupts the mind. It's really cool watching TV again and having a pizza."

"I'm so pleased that you're enjoying yourself, Dear. But how do they keep themselves entertained?" Deirdre asked.

"Well, Anton reads these weird Hindu books, and sometimes he plays this musical instrument which looks something like a guitar, but is much bigger with lots of strings and knobs, and gives off this weird sound."

"It's probably a sitar," Deirdre said. "Do they go out at all?"

"Naw. They're mostly in the house. I don't sit around with them much. I mostly stick in my room reading my Harry Potter books. Sometimes, I'm even glad to get away to school."

"Do you like your new school?"

"S'all right. But not as good as Holyfield. The kids there

are a rowdy bunch and the teachers are totally useless. But it's better than being at home."

"Oh dear, I'm so sorry. You were happy at Holyfield, and I know the school very well, after having taught there for so long."

"Yeah," Kevin said. "And another thing, Anton's got Mum hooked on drugs now."

"My goodness!" Deirdre exclaimed. "When did this happen?"

"Dunno. Since they came back from India, I suppose. Mum used to have a joint before, sometimes, but now it's sort-of regular. They sit and smoke this ganja stuff and become all stupid and dopey."

"Well, I'm not too surprised, Dear. I somehow felt that Anton was into drugs. His whole demeanour suggested it, and marijuana is so easily available in India. Where does he get his supplies from here?"

"From his weirdo friends, I guess," Kevin said. "They all smoke it after their puja in a pipe sort of thing that they pass round the circle."

"Oh dear," Deirdre said to herself. It's drugs now. Not a very suitable environment for an impressionable child, like Kevin.

It was half-past-ten before she told Kevin to go to bed. "I'll come up later and tuck you in."

"Cool," Kevin said.

When she was downstairs again, after the bedtime ritual, she poured herself a stiff Scotch from the drinks cabinet, and settled herself into her armchair. Timothy got down from the sofa and jumped up on her lap, purring madly. She worried about Kevin and the environment he lived in.

It was so marvellous having him back in her household again, and he seemed to be so happy being with her. Why had she allowed herself to become so attached to him? When Sharon first arrived to live with her, she never imagined she would become so fond of Kevin — or any child for that matter. Love in her life had been sadly lacking — except for Howard and her parents, of course. However, that was a different sort of love.

The next day, Deirdre decided to cook a roast beef dinner, so she busied herself in the kitchen while Kevin played in the garden or sat in the front room watching television. It was a fine meal and it came with all the trimmings — Yorkshire pudding, roast potatoes and parsnips, with carrots and broccoli. When they sat down at the table, Kevin wolfed down his food with relish, although she noticed he pushed the carrots and broccoli to one side.

"Wonder what Anton would say if he knew I was eating one of his sacred cows!"

"I don't think he would be very pleased, Dear," Deirdre said and laughed.

The next day, Kevin asked Deirdre if she would take him swimming.

"There's no pool in the village, but we can go in to Cambridge where they have a leisure centre with a heated swimming pool."

"Let's do that then," Kevin said. "Do you swim, De-De?"

"Goodness, no." Deirdre said. "Not at my age, Dear. But I used to swim quite well when I was young. Do you have any swimming trunks with you?"

"Yeah. I brought them in my overnight bag—just in case."

When they reached the leisure centre, Deirdre waited while Kevin changed in the locker room, and emerged from the showers, dressed in his red swimming trunks. She sat on a bench at the side of the pool while Kevin jumped in and splashed in the water with all the other children. He could swim quite well, and looked like a little fish with goggles. Sometimes, he would show off and call out to her "De-De, look at me. I'm going into the deep end now."

"Don't go too far, Dear," Deirdre said. She looked around anxiously to make sure that a lifeguard was nearby.

Kevin's unexpected holiday came to an end all too soon, when Anton came to collect him the same evening.

"I hope you haven't been too bored over the holiday weekend, because we haven't done very much." Deirdre sought reassurance.

"It's been cool," Kevin said, "just talking to you, De-De. Can I take my bike back with me this time?"

"Of course you may, Dear. It's your bike, after all."

He gave Deirdre a big kiss and a huge hug, then wheeled his bike from the garage and joined Anton, who had waited at his combi.

Chapter 12

The following few weeks dragged on. Deirdre tried to busy herself with routine chores. She did not undertake the house-cleaning, as 'dear Mrs Dunwoody' came around regularly to dust, vacuum and clean. Deirdre was quite content to brush any offending crumbs or debris temporarily under the carpet. A big house like hers needed a lot of upkeep, as her bric-a-brac and books were dust collectors, and Timothy did not help with his cat hairs.

Her thoughts mainly centred on Kevin and the sort of life he had to endure with his mother and new stepfather. He seemed neglected, and, she thought, unloved. Perhaps that was why he had formed such a close attachment to her.

It was strange, she reflected, that the young and the old could bond so closely. Grandparents, for instance, always seemed to have more time and affection for their grandchildren than for their own children, and indulged in them more. Perhaps, this was because they were relieved of much of the responsibility for the child's upbringing. Anyway, she had no grandchildren, so she supposed that she had found a substitute in Kevin.

There had been no news of him for a few weeks now, but late one wet and windy afternoon, as she settled down to a cup of tea beside the log fire, the doorbell rang. Waiting outside the front door with his bicycle was Kevin!

"Good gracious, child," she said in astonishment, "this is an unexpected surprise. What on earth are you doing here?"

"I've run away from home," he said, taking off his helmet.

"My dear, you'd better come on inside. You're soaked to the skin."

Kevin propped his bicycle on its stand and came into the house.

"What on earth has happened?" Deirdre said.

"Aw, I'm just fed up with those two weirdo's," he said. "I can't take it anymore." He took off his backpack and wet windcheater and hung them on the coat-stand beside the door.

"Does your mother know you're here?" Deirdre asked, anxious lest this cause a lot of trouble. As if in answer to her question, the telephone in the hallway rang and Deirdre picked it up from the hook. It was Sharon.

"Is Kev with you?" she asked. "I think he's done a runner."

"He's just arrived here, as a matter of fact," Deirdre said. "I think he's ridden all the way on his bicycle."

"Oh, that's good. At least we know where he is," Sharon said. She did not sound unduly concerned.

"I had better bring him back home straight away," Deirdre said.

"Naw, just leave him to cool off. He'll be okay with you, if you don't mind having him for a day or two. Anton can go and fetch him. At least we know where he is, so we don't have to inform the police."

Deirdre took Kevin into the living room. "You had best warm yourself beside the fire," she said. "You're as cold as ice—and wet. Did you ride all the way?"

"Yeah," Kevin said. "It's only fifteen miles."

"Still, that's a long way, especially in this weather. You had better go upstairs and get out of your wet things. Did you bring any dry clothing with you?"

"Yeah, some jammies and a few things in my backpack."

"Well, you do that, Dear, while I make you a hot cup of soup. Would you like a sandwich?"

"Naw, just a slice of bread and butter."

"I'll bring them up to you," Deirdre said, "Then I think you should have a nice hot bath to warm you up."

"Okay," Kevin said. He was such an obedient child, at least when he was with Deirdre. He collected his backpack and went upstairs.

When Deirdre took him his soup and bread, he was already in his pyjamas, sitting on the edge of his bed. She went into the bathroom and filled the tub with hot water. She didn't have his favourite bubble-bath so used some of her own.

"Now, pop into the tub, Dear, while I take your wet things and dry them beside the fire. Call me if you need anything."

"You'll do my back?"

"I will indeed. Just call me when you're ready."

As Deirdre finished hanging Kevin's wet clothing on the clotheshorse, which she had placed before the fire, she heard him call out from the landing.

"I'm ready, De-De."

He was already back in the tub surrounded by foam when she entered the bathroom.

"What caused you to run away?" Deirdre asked as she soaped his back with the sponge.

"I'm just fed up. They're both on at me all the time — Anton telling me off and Mum nagging. And they fight a lot. They just had a blazing row before I left. I don't like it there, De-De. Can't I come and live with you?"

"I'm afraid not, Kevin dear. You'll have to go back when Anton comes to collect you."

When she finished scrubbing Kevin's back, he stood up in the tub and, to her horror, Deirdre noticed ugly bruises on his bottom.

"My goodness! How did you get these?" Deirdre said in a shocked voice.

Kevin craned his neck so that he could peek at his behind.

"Oh, those? That's Anton."

"What on earth did he do to you?"

"Well," Kevin said, "the other day he caught me messing around with his beads and stuff, and he went totally ballistic. He said I was defiling his holy stuff, and he hauled me across his knee and whacked me really hard."

"How many times?"

"Dunno. I lost count. But it hurt."

"What did your mother have to say?"

"Mum? She wasn't in the house and she doesn't know. I haven't told her. If I say anything, there'll be another blazing row and I don't want to stir things up."

"I think she *should* know," Deirdre said.

"Naw, it's better that she doesn't."

"I am quite shocked, Dear. I had no idea Anton was so violent. I thought being a practicing Hindu he would be more peaceful and gentle."

"Naw, he flies into terrible rages when he's upset, especially if it's about his sacred stuff. His eyes go red and bulgy—like a mad dog's balls, and he lashes out. He even hit Mum once, and gave her a black eye. He's a real weirdo, and I really hate him."

"I quite understand, Dear. Now, you get some rest. You look exhausted."

When he had stepped out of the tub, she dried Kevin off with a soft bath-towel. She wrapped this around him and led him to his bedroom, where she helped him into his pyjamas. Then she tucked him into bed.

I'll bring you up a nice hot cup of Horlicks later, if you're still awake."

"I'd love cocoa, please."

She went downstairs and poured herself a stiff Scotch. Her nerves felt frayed and she was tense and angry. Anton seemed a dreadful person, and his demeanour belied his true nature. Fancy mistreating a child like that! She would ring

Mildred in the morning and seek her advice. Mildred would know what to do.

Before going to bed, Deirdre peeped into Kevin's room to see if he was awake for a hot drink, but he was fast asleep.

The next morning, he was hot and feverish. "Stay in bed today, Dear. I'll bring you some warm milk and a hot-water-bottle."

Oh dear, she thought, I hope it's nothing serious. She took his temperature in his bottom, using her rectal thermometer, the only one she had. When she was a child, her mother always took her temperature this way as she had a holy terror that the thermometer would break in the child's mouth and the deadly mercury be swallowed. He made a bit of a fuss at first, but in the end consented, and pulled down his pyjama bottoms. The thermometer registered 102°F when she took it out. Later, when she took it again, it had climbed even higher. She got on the phone to 'dear Doctor Wilson.'

"The doctor can't come immediately," the receptionist told

her. "You may have to wait till evening. But if the child's temperature becomes higher, it will be best to send for an ambulance to take him to hospital."

However, the doctor was able to make a home visit earlier than anticipated. He examined Kevin's chest with his stethoscope. "There doesn't appear to be any fluid on his lungs," the doctor said, "but his temperature is quite high. It's probably just a bad chill, but if it's not better by the morning, it may be wise to send for an ambulance and have him admitted to A&E." He prescribed Paracetamol, told Deirdre to keep him warm in bed, and give him plenty of fluids to drink.

She sat with Kevin for a while, reading to him from his book, while he sniffled, sneezed and coughed, then she left him to go to sleep. Throughout the night, she went into his bedroom and felt his head with the palm of her hand while he slept. Fortunately, he was better the next morning, and when she took his temperature again, it had come down.

This came as a great relief to Deirdre as she had a holy

terror of sickness, remembering the time when, as a child, she had run the gauntlet of childhood illnesses, like mumps, measles and chicken-pox. Fortunately, now-a-days, these common childhood illnesses were prevented by vaccination. Also, in England, you were safe from the terrible tropical diseases like malaria, smallpox, typhoid and cholera, which ravaged India. In Kevin's case, it seemed that it had just been a bad chill, probably due to his exposure to the elements during his fifteen-mile cycle ride in the cold and wet. She hoped he would soon be up and about again after a few days' rest.

Chapter 13

Deirdre called her friend Mildred, at Social Services, the following morning, while Kevin was still asleep. She related the events to Mildred in as much detail as possible.

"It seems a clear case of physical child-abuse," Mildred said. "You will need to bring him in as soon as possible for a physical examination by a paediatrician, and a report will have to be filed."

"I shall do so immediately, as soon as Kevin is better. He is in bed with a severe chill. What will all this involve?" Anxiety laced her tone.

"Well, he will be given a thorough medical examination, which might entail an investigation into possible sexual abuse."

"Oh dear," Deirdre said. "I hope Kevin will not find all this too traumatic."

"Well, it's usually done routinely in cases like this. So

many children, who are physically abused, are sexually abused too. Of course, it may not happen."

Mildred worked at the Social Services Office based in Cambridge. So, once Kevin was better a few days later, and up and about again, she bundled him into the car and off they drove. On the way, she explained to Kevin what was happening.

"Can't we leave it be, De-De?" He looked stricken. "I don't want to make a big thing out of this. It'll only stir things up and cause a lot of trouble. I'm okay, and the bruises will soon clear up."

"That is why we have to act quickly, Dear, while there is still some evidence to show that you have been ill-treated."

"Yeah, I suppose. But it's going to cause a lot of hassle."

"Yes, I understand, Dear. It was different in my day, when children were quite often spanked by their parents or caned by their teachers, but a lot has changed in recent years, and now-a-days abuse of children is not tolerated."

"Yeah, I've never been whacked like that before. Mum used to give me a slap on the bum sometimes when I misbehaved, but it never hurt much and I guess I deserved it."

When they arrived at the Social Services Office, Mildred explained to Deirdre the formalities and procedures that would be necessary — form filling, interviews, a physical examination, reports, and a possible court order to remove Kevin from the custody of his parents.

"But, who would he be placed with? Would he have to be put into care?"

"It is quite likely that he will be put into your custody, for the time being, if you will have him. We would be hard-pressed to find someone else as suitable as you to place him with. Are you prepared to take on the responsibility?"

"I would be more than happy to take charge of Kevin, as you know, Dear."

After all the procedures had been gone through and on their return journey home, Deirdre asked Kevin how he had fared during the examination.

"Well," he said, "they made me strip naked and took lots of photographs and measured the bruises, and wrote things down. Then they made me lie on the table and poked and prodded me all over—even in my bum-hole. It was totally embarrassing! They asked me stupid questions, like had Anton touched me. I said, of course he fucking touched me, can't you see the marks?"

"I think they meant a different kind of touching, Dear."

"What do you mean?"

"Fondling your genitals—your private parts," Deirdre explained.

He looked out the passenger window and fidgeted. "No, Anton's never done anything like that, even though he's a total weirdo. I wish, now, you hadn't seen the marks," he mumbled, "then there wouldn't have been all this hassle."

"It's for the best, Dear. If he's allowed to get away with abusing you this time, he'll only do it again, and on the next occasion he may damage you even more severely."

"What's going to happen now?"

"Well, it's likely that you will be removed from the custody of your parents—your mother, I mean. They might consider her an unfit parent and that you are at risk from Anton. Did you mention they were on drugs?"

"Yeah. They asked me questions like that. I said they sometimes smoked a joint together. But if I'm taken away from them, what's going to happen to me?"

"Well, Dear, it's quite possible that you may be placed in my care."

Kevin's voice brightened. "What? Really? That's cool. I'd love to live with you!"

"It all depends on the results of the tests and reports," Deirdre said. "It will take a few days before we know for certain."

"If that's what's going to happen, then it's been worth all the hassle."

Deirdre reached over and patted his knee, as tears filled her eyes.

Three days passed before Sharon phoned again. After perfunctorily asking how Kevin was, Sharon said that Anton would be picking him up that evening.

"I'm afraid that won't be possible," Deirdre said. "Anton has mistreated Kevin and it has been reported to the authorities. There is likely to be a court order removing him from your custody."

"Mistreated him? In what way?"

"He has some very nasty bruises on his bottom."

"What do you mean? Has Anton whacked him?"

"Yes, I'm afraid so. He has had to have a physical examination, and it's all in the hands of the authorities now. There's likely to be an Emergency Protection Order issued."

"I'm sure Anton didn't do anything like that," Sharon said. She sounded aggressive. "Kev might have hurt himself falling down or something. He tells terrible lies sometimes, and he's manipulative. He's certainly twisting you around his little finger."

"I'm sure Kevin is not making it up," Deirdre said in a firm tone. "And his account of what happened has been officially reported and filed."

"Where is he going to stay?" Sharon asked, even more aggressively.

"Well, temporarily, it's likely he will be placed in my charge."

"You'd like that, wouldn't you?" Sharon said. The spite in her voice came through loud and clear. "You've always wanted to take Kev over. Whenever he's been with you, he comes home completely spoiled and behaves like a total brat. That's probably why Anton lost his rag with him. He probably deserved it anyway. He needs the firm hand of a man sometimes."

"Yes, but not to whack him with!" Deirdre said, trying to conceal the anger in her voice.

Sharon raised her voice. "Well, we want him back!"

"I'm afraid that won't be possible," Deirdre said, remaining firm. She was quite surprised at her own resolve.

Usually, she was rather cowardly in such situations. But here, Kevin's welfare was at stake. "The issue is out of my hands now and, in all likelihood, Anton may be prosecuted for physical child-abuse."

"What? For just a smack?"

"It was not just a smack. Kevin's bottom is black and blue all over. Anyway," she continued, "I don't see any point in prolonging this conversation. There is nothing more to say."

With that, Deirdre put the phone down. Her pulse raced, but at least she had stayed firm.

Chapter 14

The next few days were busy ones for Deirdre. She was on the phone to Mildred on a daily basis to ascertain how the situation was progressing with regard to Kevin. Deirdre also felt concerned that Kevin's only possessions were the clothes he stood in. It was Kevin's main worry too.

"What's going to happen about all my stuff, De-De? There are all my toys and books, and I miss my laptop and X-box. I know you're washing my clothes on a night, but I'm still fed up of wearing the same stuff every day."

"I'll speak to Mildred, Dear. You will probably be assigned a social worker, and arrangements can be made for her to visit your parents and collect your things. So, it would be a good idea if you wrote down what you have so that she'll know what to ask for. In the meanwhile, I'll take you to Marks tomorrow and get you a few things to tide you over — at least a change of clothing and some underwear."

They shopped in Marks and Spencer in Cambridge the following day. Deirdre bought him two pairs of jeans, a couple of t-shirts and four pairs of sleeveless vests and y-fronts. She also purchased him a new pair of trainers, as his were worn out, and six pairs of socks. His windcheater was in a bad state too and, now that they were well into autumn and the weather was becoming colder, she got him a new one that would keep him warm and snug. At his pleading, she also got him a baseball cap with a Nike symbol on it. She did not baulk at the expense, as she was comfortably off financially and her own needs were few.

Kevin was pleased with all the purchases, and it was a novelty for Deirdre, shopping for clothes for a child for the first time. The shopping done, they went to McDonalds for hamburgers and fries, and a thick shake for Kevin. Deirdre had a coffee.

A few days later, Deirdre had another call from Sharon. "Anton and I would like to come over and speak to you and

Kev."

"I don't think that would be appropriate under the circumstances, Sharon. There is no point in talking to me, and as far as Kevin is concerned, you will not be allowed to see him except in the presence of a social worker."

"Yeah, I had a letter from Social Services. It's wrong of them to keep me away from my own child, and Anton is totally furious about all this. He said Kev was desecrating his sacred things and he lost it for a while. But he says he's sorry he whacked Kev. We can bring some of his stuff over at the same time. I don't know how he's survived without his laptop all this while."

"That won't be necessary," Deirdre said stiffly. "The authorities are arranging for a social worker to visit you and collect his things. I would be obliged if you could pack them in a box and have it ready for her when she comes."

"Yeah," Sharon said. "I'll see what I can do. But I really wanted to talk to you and see if we can sort all this out between ourselves."

"It's too late for that now, and the matter is completely out of my hands," Deirdre said. "As such, there is no point in discussing it any further."

The tone of Sharon's voice changed. "Well, if that's your attitude and you're so bloomin' fond of Kevin, you're welcome to him. You haven't seen him when he plays up. He can be a total pain. He's been a millstone round my neck ever since I had him, and besides, I have a new baby on the way — Anton's and mine, so the best of British luck!" With that, she rang off.

The social worker appointed for Kevin was a young woman called Hillary. She came to visit Deirdre, and also spoke to Kevin. She had a look around the house, particularly at Kevin's bedroom. Kevin gave her the list of things he had written down in his scribbly handwriting, and she promised to get them for him. "Don't forget my laptop and X-box," he said as she left.

Kevin was re-admitted to Holyfield school, and Deirdre

took him down to speak with his head teacher, Mr. Stewart. She explained the circumstances and informed him she had been appointed as Kevin's guardian for the time being.

Kevin was happy going back to his old school again, and life fell into a routine pattern. Hillary came around with Kevin's things, and he was relieved to have them all back. Hillary said there was some trouble in trying to get Kevin's laptop, as Sharon claimed that it was really hers and Kevin was just using it. But, eventually, she was able to regain possession of it on her insistence.

Then Mildred phoned and told Deirdre that there was going to be a court hearing about Kevin, and that she was required to attend, as were Sharon and Anton.

This took place the following week, and when they sat in the courtroom, Sharon was dressed more soberly than usual, and Anton sat beside her, with a vacant expression on his face. He too was dressed more conventionally, lacking his tunic and beads, but with his hair still in rat's tails. After a brief hearing, the judge ruled in favour of giving Deirdre custody of Kevin, until further reports could be examined. Mildred and Hillary attended the hearing too.

On the way out of court, Sharon did not attempt to speak to Deirdre, but gave her a scathing look as she and Anton drove off in their combi. Deirdre noticed the bulge in Sharon's stomach. What sort of life is that poor unfortunate child going to have? Deirdre asked herself, with a shake of her head.

Chapter 15

It had not been necessary for Deirdre to contact Mildred so frequently on the phone, now that Kevin's affairs had been temporarily settled. But, one day, she had a call from her saying she would like to see Deirdre at her office.

She got in her car and drove to Cambridge and parked at the Social Services offices. Mildred sat at her desk, speaking on the telephone, when Deirdre entered. She gestured to her to sit down.

After a couple more minutes, she ended the call and turned her attention to Deirdre. "I would like to discuss Kevin's medical examination report with you," she said, then passed a paper to Deirdre. "This is the report on his physical examination. You will see from it that there is some indication of sexual abuse. It is not recent, but has possibly happened sometime in the past."

Deirdre had a look at the paper. It was mostly in medical

jargon, but Deirdre noticed some comments like, 'No bruising around anal area,' and 'some indication of anal reflex dilation and scarring.'

"Oh dear," Deirdre said, "what does all this mean?"

"Well, it means that it is likely that Kevin has suffered some sexual molestation in the past, although it is by no means conclusive. How long ago was it that Kevin first went back to live with Sharon and Anton?"

"Let's see," Deirdre said. "It wasn't long after his tenth birthday, so that would be about three months ago."

"It's not clear how long ago this might have happened," Mildred said, "so there's nothing to prove Anton was the possible abuser. Kevin also denied that Anton had molested him sexually in any way when he was questioned about it."

"Yes, he told me that too," Deirdre said.

"Well, perhaps you could try to find out from Kevin?"

"Oh, I don't know, Dear. I think he would be unwilling to tell me anything. He did mention that in the past Sharon had left him with friends, when she went away with a new boyfriend on a weekend spree."

"It may very well have happened then," Mildred said. "Emotional scars last longer than physical ones, so is it possible that you could try and find out? It would be very helpful, and would take Anton out of the equation, if nothing else."

"I'll do my best, Dear," Deirdre said, "But I can't promise."

On one of their autumn walks, Deirdre felt it was an appropriate time to broach the subject. "Kevin dear," she began, "remember when you told me that when the doctors were examining you they asked you certain questions about Anton's behaviour towards you — in a sexual manner, that is."

"Yeah?" Kevin said.

"Well, Dear, they seemed to have found evidence that at some time or other, you might have been sexually interfered with. Did this ever happen, and could you talk to me about it?"

Kevin remained silent for a minute. He kicked at some

fallen leaves on the ground. "I can talk to you about most things, De-De," he said eventually.

"Can you not talk to me about this?"

"Well," Kevin said after some deliberation. "It happened a long time ago. You see, Mum used to leave me with these friends when she went away with her boyfriends. Well, there was this thirteen-year-old who was their son. I used to have to sleep in his room, and he messed around with me."

"In what way, Dear?"

"Well, he used to get me to do things for him, and he used to do things to me."

"What sort of things?"

"Blow jobs and stuff. You know what a blow-job is, De-De?"

"Yes, I'm familiar with the term, and understand what it means. And what did he do to you?"

"Well, I don't want to say, but he was big, you know, and it hurt a lot."

Deirdre formed her own conclusions of what he implied. "Did you tell your mother about this?"

"Naw, she wouldn't have believed me, and I don't talk to her about this sort of stuff anyway."

"And did this happen often?"

"Yeah, she left me with these friends quite a few times, and this boy wouldn't leave me alone. I tried to get him to stop, but he was stronger than me. I was only seven."

"Well, thank you for taking me into your confidence and being so frank with me. I'm so sorry you had to go through all this, and at such a tender age."

"Yeah, I suppose. But I don't think about it much."

The poor child, Deirdre thought. But she wouldn't reveal this to Mildred. There was no point. The boy would be too young to prosecute anyway. Of course, Deirdre was aware that these sorts of things went on between children, but she was angry that a boy — probably reaching puberty — should take such advantage of a younger child. Best let sleeping dogs lie and not stir things up, as Kevin had wanted in the first place. At the end of the day, she thought, a child went through more traumas because of all the investigative procedures that sexual-abuse involved, rather than by the act itself.

"Does all this make me a homo—a faggot, I mean?" Kevin asked.

"I'm sure it doesn't, Dear," Deirdre said in an effort to reassure him. "What makes you ask?"

"Well, the boys at school say that if you let other boys mess around with you, you're a faggot."

"Children can say the unkindest things, Dear. You went through a very nasty experience, and as you say, you don't think about it now. But should anything like that ever happen again, you will tell me, won't you?"

"Yeah, I guess so."

"You see, Dear," Deirdre continued, "there are many people—mostly adult males, who try to entice young children into sexual activity. That is why we were worried about

Anton. It is against the law and is punished very severely."

"Does this mean I'm a criminal then?" Kevin said. There was a hint of bravado in his tone.

"Oh no, Dear, not at all. You were the innocent party to all this, so you must not blame yourself in any way at all."

"Why do grownups muck about with young kids anyway?" Kevin asked, throwing a stone at a tree.

"Well, Dear," Deirdre said, "there are some people who prefer sexual contact with children. They are known as paedophiles."

"Yeah," Kevin said, "I have heard the boys talk about 'pedos.' They say things like 'he's a real pedo' — things like that."

"You don't have anyone in school who is that way inclined, do you, Dear?" Deirdre asked.

"The gym teacher, maybe. I've heard some of the boys talk about him and snigger. I don't think it's true, because he seems a regular sort of guy."

"Well, Dear, if there is any truth in this, please let me

know, don't stay quiet. This is a technique paedophiles use, to swear a young child into secrecy whilst abusing them."

"You won't tell anyone about what I've told you, will you, De-De?"

"No, Dear," she replied. "It will remain strictly between ourselves."

Back at home, Deirdre made herself a cup of tea. Kevin was in his bedroom with his laptop. She hoped he was not able to gain access to anything unsuitable for children. There was so much porn on the Internet, she had heard, and she hoped Sharon had applied some parental controls.

Children were so vulnerable these days to sexual predators, she thought. Today, it was on the news and in the papers almost on a daily basis, and was difficult to avoid. Thankfully, parents were so much more aware of sexual predators, and took the trouble to warn children about them. How different in her day, when the subject was never ever talked about.

However, this protectiveness had its downside too. Children did not have the freedom she had enjoyed as a child, when they got up to all sorts of mischief without constant parental supervision. Now-a-days, children could not even play in the park or walk alone on the street without an accompanying adult. But, she was so pleased Kevin had unburdened himself to her. She seemed to have gained his trust and confidence, and he was able to tell her about his upsetting experience. The emotional scars of sexual molestation so often outlasted the physical effects, and she was glad that Kevin seemed to have put this unpleasant event behind him.

Chapter 16

Since most of the problems concerning Kevin's future had been ironed out, Deirdre felt more comfortable in her mind. Kevin too seemed happy, and when he was not on his laptop or playing with his X-box, they went for walks down country lanes, where autumn leaves lay thick on the ground. They even caught tiddlers in the stream, and put them in the pond in the garden.

"They'll be company for Isaac and the frog," Kevin said. "I'm going to name him Freddie, when I see him."

"Yes, Freddie the frog. That's a nice name."

"Can we get some goldfish too? Pleeease, De-De?"

"We will indeed," said Deirdre. "We'll go into Cambridge tomorrow and get some. I used to keep goldfish in the pond before, you know, but they attracted a heron, and I'm afraid he gobbled them all up."

"I hope it doesn't come back and eat Isaac," Kevin said with a worried frown.

"We will get some netting at the pet shop and cover the pond," Deirdre said. "That will stop the heron from eating any of the fish—or Isaac."

As promised, Deirdre took Kevin in the car to the Aquapets shop in Cambridge the next day, and they chose six goldfish. While they were there, Kevin spotted some colourful fish swimming about in a tank.

"Can we get some of these too?" Kevin asked.

"I'm afraid those are not suitable for ponds, Kevin dear. They are tropical fish, and need to be kept in an aquarium."

"Can't we get one, De-De?"

"Oh, I don't know Dear. Tropical fish are very delicate and need a lot of care. The tank also requires regular cleaning and maintenance." A look of disappointment passed over Kevin's face.

"I'll look after it for you. I promise."

"Well, Dear, if you will take on the responsibility, then I think it is a splendid idea to have one in the conservatory."

She spoke to the man in the shop, and he showed Deirdre a variety of aquariums, and she and Kevin selected one that came with a painted, white cast-iron stand. Then they chose a pair each of colourful tropical fish — angelfish, neon tetras, guppies, kissing-gouramis, and zebra fish, as well as the six goldfish for the pond.

She also had to buy all the ancillary equipment for the fish-tank, such as an air pump, filter, thermostatically controlled water-heater, etc. Not to mention the need for some aquatic plants and gravel for the bottom of the tank. In addition, Kevin chose a fish-tank ornament in the shape of a sunken pirate ship, and then he spotted some Sponge-Bob aquatic ornaments.

"Can we have one of these too?" He asked, and tugged at her arm. "He'll be at home with all the fish and stuff around him."

"Of course we shall," Deirdre said. "Choose whichever one you like."

The shop assistant helped Kevin load all the equipment

into the boot of the Clio. The fish, in clear plastic bags filled with water, he placed in a plastic bin for Kevin to carry on his lap. Deirdre thought she had better buy a book on keeping tropical fish, so she chose one from the bookshelf.

Oh dear, Deirdre thought as they drove home in the car. And we only went into the shop for a few goldfish!

Back home and with Kevin's help, Deirdre fitted up the fish-tank in the conservatory, and filled it with water. Then Kevin installed the equipment for the tank, which he seemed to know more about, after which he emptied the tropical fish into the tank from their temporary containers. When it was all complete, they switched on the lights of the tank, and the fish looked pretty as they swam about in their new home.

"Gosh, they're awesome," Kevin said. "Thank you, De-De." He planted a kiss on her cheek.

"You're most welcome, Dear. They do look splendid, and it is so relaxing to sit and watch them swimming about, don't you think? Now, you had better put the goldfish in the pond.

We will cover it with the netting in the morning."

Kevin's love for pets and animals did not end with the fish-tank. Next, it was two birdcages — one with a pair of canaries, and the other with two little budgies. Then it was a hamster and a rabbit, both kept in hutches in the back garden. The rabbit he called Bunty, and the hamster Hamie. Kevin attended to them diligently, feeding them every day with carrots and lettuce leaves and other suitable pet food.

Deirdre was pleased Kevin had more interests now, besides his laptop and X-box. The poor child had never been allowed to keep any pets due to Sharon's aversion to animals, and the fact that they never had a permanent home, moving from pillar to post.

She and Howard had never kept any pets. She only acquired Timothy after Howard's death. But, she remembered her childhood days when their home in India was like a menagerie, with cats, dogs, chickens and ducks. She even had a pet mongoose.

Deirdre was aware that she tended to over-indulge in Kevin, and she hoped she was not spoiling him by pandering to his whims and fancies. It gave her pleasure to see him thrilled and happy. He had been a deprived child of not only love, but also of the many things his mother was not able to give him.

His happiness and well-being were her main concern these days, and being a generous person by nature, she felt it a gratifying experience. She felt that the day would come when she would have to be more assertive, but gentle persuasion had always been her tactic, rather than being strict and inflexible. Also, Kevin had been cooperative and obedient, and he minded her when she coaxed him into carrying out her wishes.

He tended to monopolise the television in the evenings, watching his favourite programs, but Deirdre was not much of a TV addict and was content to sit in the kitchen and watch the news and other programs that Kevin thought boring. After she had put him to bed, she was able to relax with a drink in front of the fire, while Timothy curled comfortably on her lap.

Chapter 17

Christmas fast approached. Instead of being heralded by angels singing, the host of TV adverts—that appeared regularly between every program—heralded it instead, starting as early as the first week in November. "Buy, buy, buy," was the keyword, and phrases like "only so-many shopping days to Christmas."

Deirdre had hardly bothered about Christmas in recent years. She usually stayed at home with Timothy, although on Boxing Day, she either visited friends, like Mildred, or invited them over. She did not bother to put up Christmas decorations, but she did light candles in the many candleholders that formed part of her bric-a-brac. One had the shape of a cottage, which when lit-up from the inside, looked pretty, with light coming through the windows. She exchanged a few greeting cards, and put the few she received on the mantle-piece. It was nice, though, to hear from absent friends—it seemed the only time of year that they bothered to get in touch.

This year would be different, she decided, seeing she had Kevin with her. She had some ideas of what to get him, but she was stuck for the 'big present' that she intended to buy for him, so she rang her friend Dave, for suggestions.

"He'd probably like a smartphone," Dave said, "provided you don't find it too expensive."

"What kind, Dear? I simply have no idea."

"One like my son's with plenty of apps and games." He suggested some makes and models, and Deirdre wrote them down on a piece of paper.

She went in to Cambridge before the shopping rush began, and chose one of the models Dave had suggested from John Lewis, after asking the shop assistant for details, trying her best to look intelligent while he explained the different features. She then shopped for Christmas decorations and a set of coloured lights and ornaments for the Christmas tree.

She preferred a natural one, rather than the artificial kind, but remembered, in fact, she already had a small coniferous tree in a pot in the garden, so she decided she would use that instead. As additional presents for Kevin, she bought him the latest Harry Potter book and some toys and games from W.H. Smith. She also bought him a Christmas stocking, already filled with various toys and treats.

She hid Kevin's presents in the wardrobe in her bedroom, so when he returned from school, there were only the decorations in carrier bags that littered the front room.

"What's all this stuff?" Kevin asked when he spied them.

"Oh, those? They're some Christmas decorations I shopped for today. I thought I would pretty the place up for Christmas.

"Cool," Kevin said. "Can I help you to put them up?"

"Of course you may. You can get the stepladder from the garage and hang up the ceiling and wall decorations. I'm getting rather too old to climb ladders these days, so your help will be greatly appreciated."

"Can we do them tonight?" Kevin asked.

"We'll start tomorrow, Dear. I am rather tired after all the shopping today."

The following day being a Saturday, Kevin was home from school to help her hang up the decorations. They started in the lounge. Kevin was up and down the stepladder, while Deirdre handed him the decorations and drawing pins to attach them with. When they had finished, the room looked quite gay and festive.

"It's just the tree now," Deirdre said. She led him into the garden and showed him the tree growing in its pot. He struggled a bit as he tried to manoeuvre it into the house, even with Deirdre helping as much as she could. It was a small tree, only about four feet tall, but the soil in the pot made it heavy. She and Kevin hung the lights and the glass balls and other decorations, including a fairy, at the top. With the help of some artificial snow, it looked pretty when they switched on the coloured lights.

"It's awesome," Kevin said, after they had finished, and surveyed their handiwork. "I've never had a Christmas with decorations and a tree and all before."

"Haven't you, Dear?"

"Naw. Mum and I always lived in these dumps, and Mum wasn't into all this Christmas stuff anyway."

"Well, this will be a change for both of us. I, too, haven't bothered much about Christmas. I think we're finished now. It's just the wreath that needs to be hung on the front door."

Deirdre left the shopping for the Christmas fare until last. She had ordered a goose from the local butcher instead of the traditional turkey. They would have that stuffed, with all the trimmings to go with it. A Christmas pudding would end the meal.

On Christmas Eve, after Deirdre had tucked Kevin into bed, she poured herself a Scotch, and then wrapped Kevin's presents. He had five of them in all, including his smartphone. She felt pleased with her efforts, as she placed them under the tree and, although they were wrapped attractively, it was rather a meagre display.

She did wonder whether it was going to be a somewhat lonely day with just herself, Kevin and Timothy. She had thought of having him attend a children's Christmas party in Cambridge, with a Father Christmas in attendance, but decided against it.

She remembered the Christmas parties she had attended in India as a child, where at the end of proceedings, there was the customary kohi-bag. This was made on a large bamboo frame, covered with kite-paper, sometimes in the shape of a fish, ship or aeroplane, and suspended from the ceiling. It would be filled with puffed rice, and mixed in was an assortment of small toys, like penny-whistles, sweets and such. As a finale to the party, someone would rip the bag apart with a long pole, and the contents would hail down; then there would be a mad scramble by the children, to find the little toys hidden among the scattered rice.

Before going to bed that night, she popped into Kevin's room while he was sleeping, and hung his Christmas stocking at the end of his bed.

Christmas morning dawned, and Kevin came into Deirdre's bedroom, dressed in his pyjamas. He hugged his Christmas stocking to his chest.

"Happy Christmas, De-De," he said, planting a kiss on her cheek. "Thank you, for your cool present."

"Happy Christmas, Dear. There are more presents for you under the tree, but you'll have to wait till after Christmas dinner before you open them."

After they had dressed and gone downstairs, Kevin spotted the presents under the tree. "Are these all for me?"

"Yes, Dear. But there's one for Timothy amongst them."

"I haven't got any present for you. I hope you don't mind."

"Of course I don't mind."

Deirdre busied herself in the kitchen for the rest of the morning, getting the goose stuffed and roasted. Then she started on the vegetables — roast potatoes, parsnips, broccoli and carrots. She hoped Kevin would eat some. Then there were the sauces and gravy to prepare, and finally, the Christmas pudding. It was all ready by midday, and they sat at the kitchen table, covered with a decorative tablecloth, and two Christmas-crackers each. A Christmas candle, decorated with holly, formed the centrepiece.

They pulled their Christmas-crackers, and put on their paper-hats. "I've got a game in mine," Kevin said. "Cool."

Deirdre indulged herself at the table, with a glass of red wine, and Kevin devoured his meal with relish (except for the carrots and broccoli). "That was scrumptious," he said. " I've never had roast goose before."

Then it was time for the presents. "I've never had so many presents before, De-De. This is really cool." He tore at the wrappings and when he finally came to his big present, he said, "Wow, awesome. A smartphone! Just what I've always wanted." He gave her a big hug and a kiss.

"I thought you would find it useful, Dear. Dave suggested it as a gift for you."

"It's awesome. Most of the other kids at school have smartphones. Now I can ring you from the playground."

They spent the rest of the day feeling thoroughly replete, and watched television. Mainly Kevin's programs. When it came to bedtime, he hugged Deirdre as she tucked him in. "Thank you, De-De," he said. "This has been my best Christmas ever."

"I'm sorry that it was just the two of us. I hope you did not find it too dull, spending it with an old lady like myself," Deirdre said.

"Of course I didn't. It was a lovely Christmas, and I love you."

Deirdre bent over and gave him an extra big kiss on his forehead. "I love you, too."

Chapter 18

Early January saw the snow lay thick on the ground, and tragedy strike. Deirdre had a phone call from Mildred.

"Deirdre, dear," she began, "I'm afraid I have some rather bad news to give you."

Deirdre was forewarned by the term of endearment, as Mildred very sparingly used the word 'dear,' unless there was bad news.

"What is it, Mildred dear?"

"I'm afraid Sharon Clarke died unexpectedly yesterday."

"My goodness! How did this happen?"

"Apparently, from a drugs overdose," Mildred said. "And it's a double tragedy, because she took the unborn baby with her too."

"This is dreadful," Deirdre said. "Kevin did mention that she and Anton were into drugs, but it was mainly softer drugs like cannabis."

"Evidently not," Mildred said. "It was most probably heroin. We will not know until the coroner's report, but that is the likely conclusion."

"Oh dear," Deirdre said. "How am I going to be able to break this news to Kevin?"

She waited apprehensively throughout the rest of the day until Kevin's return from school, fortified by several Scotches from the drinks cabinet to steady her nerves.

"Kevin, my dear child," she said, once Kevin had returned from school and hung his backpack on the hat-stand beside the door. "You'd better come inside and sit down. I'm afraid I have some very bad news to give you." She took him into the kitchen and waited until he had settled down.

"What's up?" he said.

She took his hands in hers. "Kevin, my dear, I am so sorry to tell you that your mother died suddenly, yesterday."

A look of utter shock crossed Kevin's face. But he didn't burst into tears as Deirdre had half expected.

"How did it happen?" he asked. His voice sounded quite even.

She felt it would be best not to mince her words. "It was apparently from a drugs overdose. We won't know for certain until the coroner's report."

"It's that fucking Anton, again," Kevin fumed. "He's the one who got her hooked on drugs—him and his weirdo friends!"

"Yes, I know, my dear. I completely understand."

"We were okay till he showed up—Mum and me, I mean. It was him and all his fucking Hindu stuff that changed her. He's a right fucking bastard."

"I know, Dear, but it won't help, blaming him. Your mother had a difficult life and was easily influenced. He obviously had a strong hold over her. It so often happens with people who feel insecure and perhaps unloved."

At this point, Kevin buried his head in his arms on the table and sobbed.

"There, there, now my dear. I know you are terribly

upset." She stroked his head. "It's all been a great shock. You must try to be brave."

"Fucking Anton."

"Now, Dear, I know I shouldn't do this, but I'm going to bring you a warm brandy and water to help steady your nerves."

She went to the drinks cabinet and poured a small measure of Hennessy from the bottle into a tumbler. When she returned to the kitchen, she poured warm water from the kettle into it.

"Now, drink this down, Kevin dear, then get to bed. I shall bring you up some supper later, on a tray. And don't feel afraid to cry. It helps so much to relieve the trauma and stress."

He gulped the drink down, and made a face. "It tastes just like medicine," he said.

"Yes, but it will do you good under the circumstances."

After he went upstairs, Deirdre poured herself another stiff Scotch. She had had rather too many during the course of the day, but the more she drank, the more sober she felt. A case of drinking oneself sober, she thought. She longed for a cigarette, but was glad she had none in the house. Oh dear, she thought, what would happen now?

Deirdre kept Kevin home from school the following day. "You can stay in bed today, my dear, if you like," she said.

"Naw," he said, "I'll get on my laptop, but I'll stay in my pyjamas."

Later in the morning, Mildred phoned again. "How has Kevin taken it?" she asked.

"Stoically," Deirdre replied. "But there were some tears. When is Sharon's funeral going to take place?"

"Well," Mildred said. "There will first have to be a post-mortem, then, once that has taken place, there will be a coroner's hearing. Funeral arrangements can be made after that."

"I wonder what sort of funeral it will be."

"Probably a Hindu one," Mildred answered, "seeing as she

and Anton were Hindu converts."

"I wonder where this will take place. The Hindus burn their dead."

"In a crematorium, I expect. Cremations in the open are uncommon in this country, although there have been some cases where it has been allowed. I am not sure. I will have to check."

"Who do you think will attend?"

"Well, Sharon did not have any family," Mildred explained. "She herself was brought up in care, and there are no known parents to speak of. But she might have some friends, and there will probably be Anton's."

"Kevin will have to go," Deirdre said, "but I think it would be inappropriate for me to accompany him."

"Oh, Hillary will take him. You need not worry about that. There will have to be a social worker with him anyway, because Anton will not be allowed to have any contact with him, except under supervision."

"I'll have to get him a dark suit. He has nothing

appropriate to wear—just jeans and such. I don't know what apparel Hindus wear at funerals, but I expect a dark suit will be suitable."

After a few weeks, when the inquest had taken place and a date for the funeral had been arranged, Deirdre took Kevin into Cambridge and, at Marks, had him fitted out with a dark suit, and shirt and tie, as well as shoes, because he only had trainers.

The inquest proved that it was indeed an overdose of drugs that had caused Sharon's death, and consequently that of her unborn baby. On the day of the funeral, Deirdre made sure Kevin was suitably dressed, and then Hillary came around in her car to collect him. When he returned later in the day, she asked him how the funeral had gone.

"It was really weird," Kevin said. "There were all these weirdo's dressed in white, clashing symbols, ringing bells and chanting. Anton was there too—and guess what? His head has been shaved. I hardly recognised him."

"Did he come up and try to speak to you at all?" Deirdre asked.

"Naw, he didn't bother. And I didn't want him to either — fucking weirdo."

Chapter 19

In the days that followed, Kevin's future had to be decided, and Mildred phoned Deirdre one morning before coming over to the house. "I have things to discuss with you, concerning Kevin's future," she said.

When she arrived, Deirdre greeted Mildred at the front door and led her into the lounge.

"I'll make us a nice cup of tea first," Deirdre said. She went to the kitchen and returned some minutes later with two cups of tea and some rich tea biscuits on a tray.

"As you know," Mildred began, while she stirred her tea. "Sharon's sudden death has changed Kevin's circumstances. He is now officially classed as an orphan, and it is likely he will be put up for adoption."

"I see," Deirdre said. "Will you be looking round for prospective parents?"

"Well," Mildred continued. "It is official policy to place an orphaned child with a couple or even a family. But, as you know, I very often disagree with official policy, and I was thinking that you might consider adopting Kevin yourself."

Deirdre had anticipated the question. Even so, she asked, "Wouldn't he be better off with a young family instead of an old lady like me?"

"Yes," Mildred said. "That would be the first preference, but there are other options to consider. The old and the young living together is not such a bad idea. As you well know, my grandmother brought me up and we could not have had a happier relationship. There is a certain bond that develops between the young and the old that seems to be more devoted and caring."

"Yes, I understand," Deirdre said. "I was extremely fond of my own grandparents, and they spoilt me terribly, much to my parents' annoyance. But, would I qualify to be an adoptive parent?"

"These days," Mildred said, "the rules for adoption are far more liberal than they used to be. Placing children with families is the ideal choice, but it is quite usual these days for adoptive parents to be single persons of either sex, or even couples of the same sex, like gays—either lesbian or homosexual. There is no bar on elderly people either, provided they are in good health."

"Yes, I have been keeping up with the news," Deirdre said, "and I'm aware of the changes. But would it be fair for Kevin to be saddled with an old lady like myself?"

"It is largely up to you, and whether you wish to take on the responsibility. As far as Kevin is concerned, I am satisfied he is happy with you and that is the important factor. By taking him into your care all this while, you have proved that you can provide a stable environment. You have good communication skills and have handled all his emotional problems with great tact and understanding."

"I'm thinking more of Kevin than myself," Deirdre said, then sipped from her cup, deep in thought. "For instance, what would happen to him if I took ill or passed on?"

"Oh, come now, Deirdre," Mildred said. "You have perfectly good health and energy, as you very well know, and

I do not think you have reached the end of your shelf-life by any means. And, as for passing on, this could happen to any adoptive parent, no matter what their age. You could very well live into your eighties, by which time Kevin would be well into adulthood."

Deirdre thought about this for a few moments, then said, "Well, Dear, if you're absolutely sure I am suitable, then as far as I'm concerned I would indeed be most happy to adopt Kevin. I have no family and no one to bequeath my property and possessions to. This has been on my mind for several years now, and it has been a worry."

"Well, there you are then," Mildred said. "You were prepared to foster him some time ago, when we thought Sharon had abandoned him. Well, this is the same sort of thing, except it is more permanent and legal."

"Yes, of course," Deirdre said, taking another sip from her cup.

"And, another important factor," Mildred continued, "is that I know Kevin will be in a *safe* environment. Vetting procedures are quite stringent these days for any prospective adoptive parent. However, we've known you well all these years, and you could not wish for a better recommendation. Of course, all the formalities will have to be gone through, but I feel sure there will be no problem in your case."

"Well, if you really consider that I would be suitable and that Kevin would be happy with me, I'm quite willing to take it on. But, I shall have to speak to Kevin first, and find out what he wants."

"Of course," Mildred said. "I am sure, though, that he would want to live with you, where he is happy and secure. It is so often the case, when placing children with adoptive parents, that there is a breakdown in the relationship and it ends unhappily for both parties. And there are so many risk factors that have to be taken into account."

The instance of Kevin's abuse from the thirteen-year-old came to Deirdre's mind. Children did not seem to be safe in any environment these days, she considered. An abusive stepfather or, for that matter, any relative or friend, did pose a risk, and she did not wish for Kevin to go through another traumatic experience. He was happy with her and she agreed with Mildred when she said he would be safe in her custody.

"I hope you do not feel that I have twisted your arm over this," Mildred said, as she stood at the door, ready to leave. "You see, my friend, I am not just thinking of Kevin. I'm thinking of you too." She put her hand on Deirdre's shoulder in an unexpected gesture of affection. "He needs you, and I think you need him. You are both good for each other."

"Perhaps my arm *needed* a bit of twisting, Dear." Deirdre said. "It helped me to make up my mind."

When Mildred had left, Deirdre was left alone with her thoughts. "Oh, Timothy. Am I doing the right thing?" she said. The cat looked at her, yawned, and jumped down from the sofa and onto her lap. She stroked his head.

Chapter 20

Deirdre broached the subject to Kevin the next day as they went for an evening walk. It seemed the best opportunity, while he was not distracted by the television or his X-box, and could give her his full attention. They walked to the village green, armed with slices of stale bread to feed the ducks that swam in the pond. It was a cold wintery day, but there was no wind. They sat on a bench at the water's edge and threw bits of bread at the ducks, which hungrily devoured them, ducking, diving and quacking.

"Kevin, dear," she began, "you know that this terrible tragedy of your mother's sudden death has placed you in a situation where you will have to be permanently cared for by the local authorities, or by someone who would care for you."

"Yeah, I know."

"Well, there are various options that will have to be considered. For example, giving you up for adoption to a family or any other prospective parents."

"Can't I just live with you, De-De?"

His immediate reply answered her question, but she still had to ask, "Wouldn't you prefer to be placed with a young family, where you would have a mother and father, and perhaps brothers and sisters?"

"Not bloody likely," Kevin answered.

"But, you did say once, Kevin dear, that you wished you had a dad, like some other children."

"Well, if he's going to be on my back and order me around like fucking Anton, then I'd rather not have one, or another kid who'd fuck around with me."

"Well, Dear, I just thought I would ask you what you thought about all this."

"I just want to be with you." He threw a piece of bread into the pond, and an expectant duck promptly dived for it.

"Are you absolutely sure? Being stuck with an old lady like me is not really an ideal environment for a young child like you. Wouldn't you rather have younger people around you?"

"I like being with you. You're the only one I can talk to and tell things that I would never tell anyone else. Why can't I just stay with you?"

"Well, it is one of the options that is being considered for your future. I just wanted to find out from you what you thought about it."

Kevin's face lit up. "Really? That's cool. I would really love to live with you. Are you sure you won't find me a pest? Mum always said I was a real pain in the bum sometimes — only she used the word 'arse'."

"Good heavens, Dear," Deirdre said, "I would love to have you. We have become such good friends. Of course," she continued, "there will be all the formalities that will have to be gone through, and it would make me your legal adoptive parent. If that is what you wish, I will tell Mildred of my decision, and we'll set the wheels in motion."

"Thank you," he said, giving her a hug. "I would love you to be my parent. You never nag me or get on my back, even when I misbehave. Would I have to call you 'Mum' or anything?"

"No, Dear. 'De-De' will do just fine. Now, come along, it's getting chill, and I am sure you'd like a nice hot drink when we get back home."

With that, they left the green, and Kevin held Deirdre's hand in his as they walked back.

Chapter 21

The formalities for Kevin's adoption dragged on. There were forms to fill, investigations, reports and interviews with both Kevin and herself. It seemed an endless process.

Oh dear, she thought. How long is all of this going to take? She remembered her childhood in India, when adopting a child was so simple and straightforward. Neighbouring the Himalayan town where she schooled, was Doctor Graham's Homes in Kalimpong, where there were many offspring from English tea-planters and native tea-garden coolies. These children were looked after by the Home and often placed for adoption. Besides this, there were also many native children who were parentless, and well-intentioned couples adopted them and brought them up. Indeed, some children were frequently sold by their mothers for a few rupees, as they did not have the resources to care for them.

In earlier times, even in Britain, it was also simpler, with orphanages like Doctor Barnardo's Homes where thousands of homeless and unwanted children were placed, many being put up for adoption. Of course, now-a-days large orphanages were closed down, and children placed in care in small groups, and brought up by carers — usually a couple, in a pseudo-family environment. Deirdre was uncertain which system was the better, as she had read so many news reports of vulnerable children suffering sexual exploitation even in what was considered a safe environment.

Kevin, too, seemed impatient. "When are they going to sort out all this stuff about me?" he demanded.

"We have to be patient, Kevin dear. These sorts of things can sometimes take a long while," Deirdre said as she served him with a pork chop, mashed potato and sweetcorn.

"Yeah, but it's taking forever," he grumbled. Then, quite unexpectedly, he asked, "De-De, why do girls bleed from their pussies?"

The sudden change in topic took Deirdre aback, but she regained her composure and said, "Vaginas — you mean."

"Yeah, them. Why do they bleed?"

"What makes you ask?"

"Well, today in class, one of the girls started yelling and crying, saying she was bleeding from her pussy — vagina, I mean. All the boys started laughing and sniggering, and the teacher took her to the medical room. I could see the back of her dress was stained with blood."

"Well, Dear, this happens to every young girl when she becomes a young lady. It's called menstruation, and is one of the first signs of puberty. Every child reaches puberty when they begin to change from childhood and mature into adults."

"I hope it's not going to happen to me," Kevin said, clearly alarmed. "I don't want to bleed from my willy — penis, I mean."

"Oh, it's different for boys," Deirdre said. "Menstruation only happens with girls."

"What happens to boys, then?"

"Well, there are certain physical changes, you see. Boys develop a lower voice and sprout an Adam's apple. Then there are some other physical changes, like the growing of facial and pubic hair."

"What's pubic?" Kevin asked.

"I'll explain it all to you when you are older, Dear, in the meanwhile finish your pork chop before it gets cold."

"Oh, yeah. I get it. Kids have to get old enough to have sex."

"That's the general idea."

Despite her years of experience in teaching sex education to teenagers, Kevin's direct questions sometimes caught her off guard. He seemed to have an insatiable curiosity about sex, but she was glad that he posed his questions to her rather than learn from smutty talk in school. Of course, she would have to talk to him about these matters when he was older, but she was pleased that he felt comfortable enough to bring up these questions. Now that she was taking on the responsibility for raising him, she would experience his unruly teenage years, and she hoped she would be able to cope with the situation.

The months passed, and winter turned to spring, and the first daffodils burst out in flames of yellow in her garden. The horse-chestnut tree was adorned with white candles. Kevin often ventured outside, looking for Isaac in the pond. He would take his smartphone with him and take photographs, which he would transfer to his laptop.

Deirdre sometimes felt amazed at the technology of the day. Children seemed so adept in coming to terms with all the electronic wizardry — and their gadgets could do all sorts of amazing things, like playing music and games, and of course, taking photographs and videos. In her day, all she had was her parents' HMV portable gramophone on which she played Bing Crosby and Frank Sinatra records.

In those bygone days, children seemed to share the same tastes in music and films as their parents. Today, they had a completely different culture and were not on the same wavelength as the older generation. In fact, she realized, a two-generation gap separated herself and Kevin.

Society was also so different. There seemed to be so much

more freedom then, compared to today, when there were so many more restrictions — ban this; ban that; ban the other. Also, children, she felt, were being wrapped in cotton-wool. Gone were the days when they were allowed to roam freely, and even do dangerous things — like climbing trees.

Now-a-days, she felt, there was too much over-protectiveness, when children were not even allowed to swing on swings or clamber on climbing frames in case they injured themselves. She remembered all the bumps and bruises she received, despite being a girl, taking part in rough and adventurous games. She decided she would not molly-coddle Kevin, and would give him room to explore and expend his natural energy.

She also noticed Kevin had developed an aptitude for art, and he would often spend time drawing and painting birds and animals — which included Bunty the rabbit, Hamie the hamster and Isaac the newt. Deirdre herself was an accomplished artist, so they spent time together with painting sessions in the conservatory, accompanied by the sounds of the birds chirruping in their cages.

Deirdre purchased a large book of art paper for him, and gave him some poster paints and brushes from her art cupboard. She was glad of this new interest, as it took him away from his X-box and other electronic gadgetry. Children, and even adults, these days seemed to spend far too much time concentrating on their gadgets — pressing buttons, and hardly communicating or interacting with others around them.

She also encouraged Kevin to run about and play as much as possible, and then there were their evening walks and talks together when she could get him into the fresh air and point out the wildlife that abounded around them — birds, rabbits, squirrels, hedgehogs and even the odd fox or two.

And so, the days passed happily, until the bombshell dropped.

Chapter 22

Deirdre received a phone call from Mildred one morning. "I am afraid there has been a hitch in Kevin's adoption proceedings."

"Oh dear," Deirdre said. "What has happened now?"

"Well, Social Services have received a letter from Anton objecting to Kevin's proposed adoption. He claims that being Sharon's husband he has a claim on Kevin, as his stepfather. You see," she explained, "he had to be contacted by the authorities for his permission to Kevin's adoption, and he has withheld his consent."

"But he doesn't want Kevin, surely? He has never liked the child."

"Yes, I think he is just being bloody-minded. He does not want Kevin, but he does not want anyone else to have him either."

"This is a real dog-in-the manger attitude," Deirdre said,

annoyance in her tone. "That poor child is being pulled from pillar to post."

"Yes," Mildred said, "but his claim will have to be investigated all the same. However, the history of his past physical abuse of Kevin will have to be taken into account. He and Sharon were married in India, I understand?"

"I gather it was a Hindu wedding," Deirdre said, "while they were staying in an Ashram in Calcutta."

"Hmmm. I wonder how legal the marriage was. For instance, if they both converted to Hinduism and it was an informal kind of marriage, the union may not be acceptable under British law, and as such, Anton would not be Kevin's legal guardian. The whole thing will have to be investigated all the same, so I am afraid this snag will hold matters up."

"Oh, Damn!" Deirdre exclaimed as she put the phone down. She wasn't given to expletives, but this situation demanded it. That Anton was proving to be a regular menace, throwing a spanner in the works just when everything was going so well. What did he want with Kevin, anyway? He had no affection for the boy, and was just being bloody-minded, as Mildred alleged. How was she going to explain this to Kevin? Perhaps she had better not. It would only make him more furious and frustrated. That poor child had been torn apart enough as it was.

So, she said nothing as she gave Kevin his tea on his return from school. She noticed that he seemed quiet and preoccupied as he nibbled his cheese-on-toast. This was rather unusual, as he generally chatted away to her about his school day.

"Kevin, Dear," Deirdre said, you seem to be rather quiet today. Is anything troubling you?"

He stayed silent for some moments, then said, "You know you told me once that if anyone tried to touch me, I was to tell you about it?

"Yes, Dear. I remember it well."

"You know this gym teacher in school—the one some of

the boys called a pedo? He made a grab at me in front today, when he was helping me onto the climbing frame. I was only wearing my gym shorts and he grabbed hold of me."

"Good heavens, Dear! Where did this happen?"

"In the gym, during PE."

"Did he try to do anything else?"

"Naw. I pushed his hand away and called him a fucking perv, and then he let me go."

"Did anyone else witness this — any of the other boys?"

"Naw. I told one of the boys though, and he said the gym teacher tried to stroke his bum one day. I thought the gym teacher was an okay guy, but I guess I was wrong."

"Oh dear, Kevin. I had better see your head teacher and report this right away, before some other poor child is molested."

A look of consternation passed over Kevin's face. "Do you really have to? Can't we just let it go? He didn't hurt me or anything, and it might have been an accident."

"No, I'm afraid not. He will have to be reported. What is

his name?"

"Mr Garson. Are you sure you have to report it? It'll cause a lot of hassle for him and for me. It's totally embarrassing and I don't want the word to get about, or the boys will call me a faggot."

"I understand, Dear. I know you have suffered a lot of trauma in the last few months, and this will probably cause you more. But this man must be stopped before he attempts to molest any more children."

Deirdre saw Kevin to school the next day and went straight to the Headmaster's office. He was a rotund balding gentleman, with a genial personality. He rose from his desk when Deirdre entered the room. "Mrs Hinton," he said. "It's so nice to see you again. What can I do for you?" He invited her to sit down on the chair opposite.

"Well, I'm afraid I have come to see you on rather a serious matter, Mr Stewart."

"Oh? And what is that?"

Deirdre came directly to the point. "My charge, Kevin,

told me last evening that your gym-master — a Mr Garson, I believe, tried to touch him yesterday in the genital area."

"Good heavens. Where did this happen?"

"In the gym, I understand."

Mr Stewart was silent for a minute while he tapped on his desk thoughtfully with a pencil. "Well, of course, this is a very serious allegation. Mr Garson has been with us for several years now, and there have been no accusations by any of the other boys of such untoward behaviour, as far as I am aware. But, of course, it will have to be investigated and reported to the police. Oh dear, oh dear, oh dear."

"Yes, I can understand your distress, but Kevin did tell me that one of the other boys he talked to said that he has also been touched, and there have been rumours between the boys about Mr Garson's conduct."

"I will have to see him directly, and it will probably result in his suspension, till the matter is investigated by the police. But, thank you, Mrs Hinton, for bringing this matter to my attention. The welfare of the children and the reputation of

Holyfield are paramount, and this matter must be sorted out immediately."

Back home and buttering a piece of toast, Deirdre reflected on how vulnerable children were these days to sexual predators. In her time at school, she had never suffered any untoward behaviour on the part of her schoolteachers, and there was never any gossip between the children of any unnatural conduct.

Of course, children in those days were reticent to discuss these sorts of things even between themselves. In addition, if there were any such incident, she felt sure it would have been swept under the carpet, though the guilty teacher would have been quietly removed. She couldn't imagine any child, in her time, having the gumption to report a teacher to the school head, or anyone else, for that matter. So, perhaps children were actually less vulnerable, these days.

Oh dear, she thought. More investigations. Now there was going to be further trauma for Kevin, as the police would likely interview him. Hasn't that poor child suffered enough? And, as for herself, she had lived a relatively trouble-free life over the last few years, and now the troubles were being piled on top of her one by one. Though, in many ways, problems were not always such a bad thing. They kept you alert and the grey-matter functioning. Many of the older folk these days suffered from dementia, which she considered was caused by an inactive brain.

She was glad, too, that Kevin had told her about the incident, and had heeded her advice. He needed someone to unburden himself to, and not keep his troubles to himself, as so many children seemed to do — instead, becoming withdrawn and reticent.

With these thoughts in her mind, she gave Timothy his cat food when he came into the kitchen, with his tail in the air, and meowed at her expectantly.

Chapter 23

As Deirdre expected, a police interview with Kevin, in the presence of her and Hillary, took place at the house. A young lady officer, who seemed sensitive and understanding while questioning Kevin, represented the police. He was not able to tell her very much, except what he had told Deirdre. She did ask him for the name of the boy who told him Mr Garson had touched his bottom, and he gave it to her. She also questioned Kevin about Mr Garson's behaviour towards the boys in the gym, but he was not able to tell her very much, except to say some of the other boys thought him a bit of a pedo.

When Deirdre phoned Mr Stewart, he informed her that the police had also interviewed him and Mr Garson. He told her that Mr Garson's contention was that his hand had accidentally touched Kevin when it slipped as he helped him onto the climbing frame.

"We will have to let matters stand as they are at the

moment," Mr Stewart said. "However, Mr Garson has been cautioned, and a very watchful eye will be kept on him. They also asked him about the other boy he was alleged to have touched on the bottom, and his excuse was that it was just a friendly pat. None of the other boys who were questioned admitted to any sexual interference, so for lack of evidence, we will have to give him the benefit of the doubt. You see, Mrs Hinton," he went on, "it is very difficult for a gym teacher not to have some sort of physical contact with the boys during PE, and such contact can often be misconstrued."

Deirdre saw the point of Mr Stewart's explanations, but she was not altogether convinced. Anyway, she was relieved at the outcome as far as Kevin was concerned. The interview with the police had not caused him too much trauma, and at least matters seemed to have been nipped in the bud. She also felt confident that Kevin would confide in her if any further untoward incidents took place.

She also had better news from Mildred, concerning Anton's application for custody of Kevin. "It appears that the marriage is not considered legal, as Anton could not produce a marriage certificate to prove that the Hindu wedding ever took place between him and Sharon. Also, his history of violence didn't put him in a favourable light. As such, his appeal was dismissed, so there is nothing now to stand in the way regarding Kevin's adoption."

Deirdre met Mildred and Hillary at 'The Soldier of Fortune' for a few lunchtime drinks to celebrate the occasion. "I am so grateful for all the help you have given me," Deirdre said, as she raised her glass. "So, cheers dears, and bless you both."

Kevin, too, was overjoyed at the news. "Gosh," he said. "You're my new mum now, De-De, and I'll always love you."

"I know, Kevin, dear, and I'll love you too. But I want to be more your friend than a mum."

"You'll always be that. I've never had a real friend like you before."

However, if Deirdre thought that her troubles were now at an end, she was sadly mistaken. One day, Kevin was late returning home from school. She did not worry too much at first, thinking he might have been kept back for detention. She tried to ring him on his smartphone, but it was switched off, so in the end, she rang the school. The school janitor answered the call. "I'll have a look around to see if he's here, if you'll hold on," he said. A few minutes later, he returned and said, "There's nobody here."

Worried, she drove toward the school, and discovered Kevin's bicycle leaning against a hedge at the side of the road, at about the halfway point. No way would Kevin abandon his bicycle. Consternation filled Deirdre as she put the bike in the boot of the car. She phoned the police as soon as she returned home, and two policemen came around to the house almost immediately.

"The fact that his bicycle has been abandoned," the police officer said, "seems to clearly suggest that he has been abducted. Do you have any idea who might have done this?"

"The only one I could possibly conceive of who would do such a thing is his supposed stepfather, Anton," Deirdre said.

"He had applied for custody of the child but was refused. He might have done this out of spite and malice."

"Did he know where Kevin went to school?"

"Yes, he has picked him up from school in the past, so he knew he attended Holyfield."

"Do you have his full name and where he lives?"

"I do not know his surname at all," Deirdre said. "But, I believe he has a flat somewhere in Royston."

After the police left, Deirdre spent a sleepless night. She was sick with worry, and even the few whiskeys she drank did not calm her nerves. She could hardly wait until morning, when she would phone Mildred and give her the news.

"I believe we have Anton's surname," Mildred said. "It would be on his application for custody of Kevin, along with his address. I will get hold of it and inform the police straight away."

Then, later in the day, much to Deirdre's joy and relief, two uniformed policemen arrived at the house, with a distraught

Kevin between them. He ran up to Deirdre and hugged her around the middle, and she embraced him. "Thank heaven you have been found, my dear, dear child," she said. "I have been frantic with worry over you."

"We found him without too much trouble," one of the policemen said. "The boy was not at the address we were given, but we found him at his abductor's mother's house where he had left him. We had a clue as to who had kidnapped him, as an old VW combi had been seen hovering around the vicinity of the school by some neighbours living opposite, and they noted down the registration number from the licence plate. The man has been arrested for child abduction."

Once the police had left, and Kevin was safely indoors with a hot cup of cocoa, Deirdre phoned Mildred. "What would have caused Anton to abduct Kevin?" she asked, truly bewildered. "He has no liking for the child, and I just cannot understand why he would have done such a thing."

"Just pure spite and malice," Mildred said. "He is

obviously a very possessive and controlling person, and seems quite irrational and unstable. Who knows what was going on in his mind?"

"Yes, a real weirdo, as Kevin often describes him. I'm just so glad Kevin has not been harmed in any way, but it has been a very distressing experience for him."

Kevin recounted what had taken place while he alternately blew into his cocoa and took sips. "I was just riding back from school," he said. "And suddenly, Anton screeched to a halt beside me, and he got out and grabbed me. I couldn't do anything, 'cos he's stronger. No one was around, and I had to leave my bike behind, just lying in the road. Has anyone found it?"

"Yes, Dear, it's safely in the garage. It was leaning against a hedge when I found it, so someone obviously placed it there."

"He just drove off with me. I tried to yell and scream, but he rapped me on the head and told me to shut up. Then he left me with that mean old bitch of a mother."

"I am sure all this must have been a most upsetting experience for you, Dear," Deirdre said. "Now that Anton has been arrested, he will probably be charged with abduction and, hopefully, he will be kept in custody and won't trouble you again."

"What did he want with me, anyway?" Kevin said. "He doesn't even like me."

"Who is to say what goes on in his mind? I can't see the purpose of it either. He probably knew he would not get away with it."

"I bet he wanted to take me to fucking India and make me a Hindu, like he did with Mum."

"It is not beyond the realms of possibility, Dear. But, look—I want you to put all this behind you now and not think about it. It has been a nasty experience and is best forgotten. Now, Dear, you have had a very strenuous time, and I think you will feel better after a nice hot bath and bed."

"You can bathe me if you like De-De," he said.

"I will indeed, Kevin dear." With that, she led him upstairs.

Chapter 24

They sat in the conservatory, Deirdre crocheting a tablemat, and Kevin attempting to draw one of the budgies, which kept moving about in its cage. The tip of his tongue protruded from the side of his mouth in deep concentration, as he tried to sketch the bird.

Peace at last, Deirdre thought, at least for the time being, until Anton's trial for child abduction took place. She hoped he would receive a custodial sentence, which would keep Kevin safe from his clutches, at least for a few years. Of course, Anton's trial would cause Kevin further trauma, but there was little she could do, in the circumstances, to prevent this. The phrase, 'the wheels of justice turn slowly but grind exceedingly fine,' came to mind.

She reflected on the year's events. How different and empty her existence had been before Sharon and Kevin crossed over the threshold and stepped into her life. She recalled her initial apprehension at taking them in. Yes, there had been traumas, tragedies and dramas, but she believed that fate had played a role in bringing everything to this conclusion.

It had completely changed her life, and she now had someone to care for and, she hoped, to care for her. She looked forward to the prospect of nurturing Kevin as he grew up. She would send him to college after he finished his schooling, and perhaps he would become a naturalist because of his fondness for animals. Then, as he progressed to adulthood, the expectation of his marriage and possibly children was another thing to look forward to. She would at last have a family — something she had lacked throughout most of her life.

She spared a thought for Sharon. That poor girl had led such a difficult life, being unloved and brought up in care. Then becoming pregnant with Kevin when she was still a child. It was no wonder that she resented being burdened with him and having to live in impoverished circumstances, without a proper home or support from a family. And, then, becoming involved with someone like that dreadful Anton, a control freak and weirdo. It was sad, too, that she died so young and so tragically.

Her thoughts returned to Kevin. He had been a deprived child, suffering from a lack of love and understanding. She hoped that she would be able to provide these and the security he needed. She feared that if she had not intervened in his future, especially under the influence of such creatures as Anton, he may very well have ended up on the streets as a junkie or even worse, as was the fate of so many youngsters who had an unstable childhood.

Then there was all the support of her friends, like dear Mildred, who had been a godsend, and whose advice and common-sense had guided her through so many of her problems. Being in her senior position with Social Services, her influence and support had been invaluable in determining Kevin's future.

If her belief in karma was true, Deirdre felt that she had now fulfilled a worthwhile purpose in her life. Previously, it was unfulfilled and unrewarding. She hoped now that her karma would be good, and she could progress along the path to enlightenment. This thought comforted her.

She put her crocheting to one side and got up from the wicker chair. "I'm just going into the garden, Dear, to water the plants. Do you want to come and help me?"

"Okay, De-De," he said, putting his drawing book down. "This fucking bird won't keep still anyway."

"We will do that then, shall we? But remember, Kevin dear," she said with a glint in her eye. "Don't water the marigolds!"

About the Author

I was born in Darjeeling, India in 1939 in the last decade of the British Raj. I attended Mount Hermon School, Darjeeling, where the celebrated playwright, Sir Tom Stoppard also once studied. I worked in Calcutta before migrating to England in 1969 where I worked in the PYE group of Industries in Cambridge, then joined the Civil Service and worked in Chessington, Surrey. I had to retire early due to heart problems but I found that retirement gave me more time to pursue my many hobbies, one of which was astronomy and the other writing, so I decided to put these two together and write my first book, "Over Our Heads". I've always had a passion for writing ever since I was a child, and won several prizes in writing competitions during my childhood and youth. My second book, "Don't Water the Marigolds" is my first attempt at writing a novel, and I am grateful to Harmony Kent for all the help, encouragement and support she has given me in completing this project.

I live out my retirement in my South London maisonette busily and contentedly with my two cats.

Website: **http://authorjamessinclair.wordpress.com/**
Twitter: **https://twitter.com/wayoverourheads**
Goodreads: **https://www.goodreads.com/JamesSinclair**

Made in the USA
Columbia, SC
02 October 2017